You Better Come Home With Me

You
Better Come Home
With Me

BY JOHN LAWSON

ILLUSTRATED BY

Arnold Spilka

THOMAS Y. CROWELL COMPANY · NEW YORK

For
C. C. L.
&
E. W. L.

You Better Come Home With Me

Chapter 1

Now the story begins with the Boy coming down the
road—down the mountain from the west—into town.
The curious thing was that no one actually saw him on
the road. He simply appeared on Main Street walking
from the west and so you know he must have come
that way. The road from the west becomes Main
Street when it reaches the town limits, and then it's
Main Street, and then it becomes the road to the east or
from the east. The other curious thing was that after-

wards some people remembered it so clearly and said so—like Mr. Glackensmith who was the Watch Man. He had only one eye and in that eye he wore all the time a black magnifying glass so that he could see the jewels in tiny watches. He could not see ten feet in front of him. Maybe one reason people believed Mr. Glackensmith about seeing the Boy come down the mountain five miles away was that he could see the heart beat in those tiny watches. Besides, they wanted so much to see the Boy in his faded blue jeans, sheepskin coat, and his blond hair.

It was Saturday night and it was late winter. It was cold, damp, and blowing colder. The Boy walked down Main Street past the Courthouse and into Mr. Nagle's store. It was a long store. It was narrow with counters on either side and almost at the back was the stove. The Boy walked all the way back and found a nice seat on the counter so that he had his feet up with knees under his chin and leaning back against some feed bags. Maybe it is the coziest thing in the world in the late winter around nightfall to sit by a stove. The fat black potbellied stove winds its hot-trembling chimney pipe up into the ceiling, while all the time you know you can't stay there forever.

The Boy sat there so still and so quiet that a new man who came in almost sat down on him and said he was sorry. The man looked at the Boy closely.

"Are you a MacDonald?" he asked.

"No sir," the Boy said.

One of the men by the stove said, "I thought he looked a MacDonald, too. Or a Wing. More like a Wing. But there aren't any Wings left except the Old Man."

"I'm looking for my brother," the Boy said.

"You're not from here," one of the men said. He meant the town, and he meant the whole world of this county separated from elsewhere by mountains on all sides.

"Have a good winter where you come from, Boy?" asked one of the men by the stove.

"Pretty much of a winter," the Boy said. "But we didn't have to start feeding till late this year."

One of the men approved, "It makes a big difference not to have to feed till late." Everybody nodded and several talked all at once about late falls and early springs both making the winter shorter except from different ends.

"Except," said the Boy, and everybody was quiet when he talked, because although he was only a boy maybe he was the only man in the family and if that were the case then he was the head of his family. It was not as if he had been a MacDonald where there were so many boys. "Except," the Boy said, "it's better to have the spring early when the hay might be gone and then the ewes need grass for milk and the cows . . . I don't think it's the same."

· 3 ·

"No, it's a good deal different," the men by the stove said and wondered privately who had been the fool to suggest that it was ever the same.

"One year," said one man, "I stopped feeding the eleventh day of March."

"One year," another man said, "I stopped feeding the fourth day of June."

There was a silence while the group waited for another extraordinary date to be mentioned.

"When you have two dates like that you can see the difference—that's a whole lot of time between."

Someone who had been thinking said it was almost ninety days. Almost everyone agreed. There was really very little left to be said. The men began to stand up and shake themselves and look down to the other end of the store where their women had been and still were talk, talk, talking about silly things. The evening was over. The men prepared themselves to leave each other and go back each to his own farm and face the winter week alone. They shook hands.

"You better come home with me," they said to each other. It was a way of saying good-bye or rather a way of parting and not saying good-bye. Everybody said it in these parts when he left anybody. "You better come home with me," they said.

Finally the Boy was almost alone at his end of the store facing the stove except for the Scarecrow who was still there and was sitting quite far back from the stove for obvious reasons. He hated to catch himself on fire. It was so embarrassing. It was so smoky. Whenever he caught on fire, people whom he hardly knew would come and pat him, pummel him; some, even, the really thoughtful ones, would jump on him to put out the fire. And then for days he would just sort of smolder-smoke.

The Boy and the Scarecrow sat there like that for a while and finally the Scarecrow got up and walked over to the Boy and held out his hand to say goodbye.

"You better come home with me," he said.

"Thank you," said the Boy and got up to go along. "It was extraordinary," the Scarecrow told someone later, "I said to him, 'You better come home with me' and he got up and he said 'Thank you' and there wasn't anything else to do." Because, of course, the Scarecrow was the most proper, the most kind, the most understanding. They went along to the Scarecrow's wagon and hitched up. The two of them rode out of town together in the quiet night with the smell of snow in the air.

The Boy thought that he had never driven so slowly. The old horse didn't seem to walk as much as he seemed to simply fall forward pulling the wagon behind him. The Scarecrow took his driving seriously—

sitting very straight with a tight grip on the reins staring straight ahead looking neither to the right nor left. He did this to keep control.

"Control," the Scarecrow liked to explain when he wasn't driving, "is the thing." It was why he always drove off the road when another wagon appeared on the horizon. "With my horse so wild, I can't take a chance on someone else's life." It was why the Scarecrow felt nervous that night riding out of town with the Boy beside him. No one had ever ridden with him before (mainly because they could walk faster), and now this boy's life was in his hands.

A turtle crossed the road. The horse for the first time lifted his feet. He didn't move faster. He just lifted his feet. The Scarecrow beamed. He did not relax. But he beamed.

"Spirited," he said between tight lips. "Gallant."

Suddenly the silence of the night was broken by a church bell from the edge of town which was still not far behind them. The Scarecrow pulled the reins up short and what little forward motion there was, was stopped.

"Listen, Boy," the Scarecrow said, "listen to the bell!" They sat still and close in the dark night and looked back down the empty road to town where in the dark night the white church was a black shadow.

The Scarecrow longed to cry out, "It's beautiful. It's beautiful." But to have said a word would interrupt the bell on its lonely way, and even a bell working slowly and steadily goes its way through ten clangs, ten bangs, ten rolling echoing ka-wangs, and then suddenly . . . is stilled. Yet they sat as they had—close, waiting, hoping that perhaps tonight there might be one last lone unconnected bang—but there wasn't. There never is. The Scarecrow shook his head sadly.

"Oh," he said. "Oh," he said. "Boy, that is a remarkable bell."

He straightened his back and put the bell and its beauty from his mind and turned to face the road.

They moved along slowly down the valley road south from town with the mountains rising in darkness on each side of them. The sky had cleared now so that here and there you were aware of the white patches of clouds racing across the sky between the mountains and then disappearing to race over the rest of the world below.

The Boy, peering ahead into the darkness, knew that he had come to the right country. For certainly up here on the top of the world where the air was so clear and the sound of a bell so clean and pure and with such people as the Scarecrow to be driving home with he would find what he had lost. It was the certainty of this—and being sleepy, too—that let the Boy close his tired, blinking eyes. He went to sleep there and then, falling against the Scarecrow.

The Scarecrow was annoyed. The Boy had put his

life in the Scarecrow's hands and was now falling asleep against him, upsetting his balance, throwing off his timing, endangering his control. And on top of it they were coming to the Straight Stretch.

The Straight Stretch is the Straight Stretch. It is that part of the road to the south which runs straight as a string for miles—and miles. It is where the boys come to race their fastest horses. It is where the drivers let go.

The Scarecrow pulled to a stop. He shook the Boy to come awake.

"Seat belt," the Scarecrow said and showed him how to fasten himself as he did the same.

"Ready, Boy," the Scarecrow shouted for the wind had suddenly come up against them. They moved forward at the very same speed as before. But there was the wind which came at them, tore at them.

"Must be doing a hundred," shouted the Scarecrow. And the Boy went back to sleep. It was unbelievable. "Nerves of iron," as the Scarecrow told his friends later. "The Boy went to sleep. Put himself in my hands going up the Straight Stretch like sixty. I'll never forget it."

Chapter 2

The Boy did not wake until almost nine the next morning when the Scarecrow shook him. The Boy sat up very straight and wondered if they were still going down the Straight Stretch and were about to have a wreck. And then, of course, he looked all around and wondered where he was.

He had awakened in the tiny little attic room where the Scarecrow had carried him the night before and tucked him in with old red and green quilts. The Scarecrow led the way down the narrow stairs to the kitchen which was warm and cozy with a small fire. A big black cookstove purred with the fragrance of French omelettes and burning toast—or was it ham and honey? There was a large table in the center of the room piled with books and catalogues and enough space cleared at either end for them to sit down.

The Scarecrow had prepared a magnificent breakfast of porridge, bacon, hot bread and apple sauce and cold milk, a French omelette and burnt toast.

"We eat very simply here, Boy," the Scarecrow said.

"It's wonderful," said the Boy. "And the porridge is a credit to you."

"Thank you."

"I apologize for falling asleep last night," said the Boy.

"You were certainly sound asleep."

"That I was." The Boy had a quaint way of talking and a foreign (Midwest) accent all of which the Scarecrow thought was very special.

They sat and ate in silence which is really the only way to eat. Then they rocked back and enjoyed the good feeling.

Finally the Scarecrow spoke. "Excuse my rocking back," he said. "I should set a better example, I know." It was at this moment that there was a knock on the door. But before the Scarecrow could even get up, the door had burst open, smoke was coming down the chimney, and a very attractive red fox in a handsome corduroy hunting jacket, Norfolk style, with a magnificent cane, strode into the room and took his place in front of the smoking fireplace.

"Aha," he said.

"Please," the Scarecrow said, "the door, please shut the door. It makes my fire smoke."

"Don't change the subject, Scarecrow," said the Fox, who did not leave his place. The Scarecrow got up and closed the door himself and then came back to the Boy.

"Ah, Mr. Fox, I want you to meet the Boy. Boy, this is Mr. Fox, one of my oldest acquaintances."

"How do you do, sir," said the Boy.

"Very good manners," said the Scarecrow aside to the Fox.

"Huumph," said the Fox. And then turning to the Scarecrow, "Well, it's lucky you have friends like me. I expected to find you—" and Mr. Fox made a cutting motion across his throat.

"Now, now, Mr. Fox, have a cup of coffee and a little burnt toast," said the Scarecrow soothingly.

The Fox strode about. "Just take up with any stranger, will you? Why I don't know a single twelve-year-old boy who isn't a juvenile delinquent these days. Hoodlums, all of them."

The Scarecrow turned to the Boy. "You must understand about Mr. Fox—he is just—uh . . ."

"That he is," said the Boy.

"Suspicious" is the word Scarecrow was looking for. Mr. Fox was suspicious—foxy, if you will. He knew there was something beneath the surface, any surface. Nothing was what it appeared and it was sure to be worse if you knew the truth. The Scarecrow was the miracle who defied Mr. Fox's Law of Suspicion. Therefore he felt absolutely bounden to protect him from the world—from strange boys like this waif boy who had appeared out of nowhere.

"Hrrruuumph," said Mr. Fox. "Boy, you go outside and look around." As the Boy started out the door, Mr. Fox winked knowingly at the Scarecrow.

"No you don't, Boy. You come back here and sit here. We'll go out." He took the Scarecrow by the arm and marched him out of doors.

They went down to the garden gate. The Fox watched the door warily. The Scarecrow disengaged himself and gazed down the valley sadly and alone, to where the mountains rolled away into a darker blue, and he wondered why some people made living so complicated. No doubt the Fox was wiser than he, but the Scarecrow did not want to be wise the way the Fox was wise. That was where the Fox was so wise he was stupid. If only he would let me be, groaned the Scarecrow. But Fox would not let him be.

"Did you see that," he said, "did you see the way he wanted to get out? He knew I was on to him.

He's smart. Clever lad. He knew I was on to him."

"He's a nice boy," said the Scarecrow firmly.

"And how did he get here?"

"I was at the store. He was at the store," said the Scarecrow. "And as I was leaving I said, 'You better come home with me.' It was the most extraordinary thing the way he simply said, 'Thank you,' and made ready to come home with me."

Mr. Fox stuck his paw deep into the Scarecrow's blue-denim-covered chest triumphantly.

"And how many times have you said 'You better come home with me'? Very queer he should take you up on it, I say."

"Well," said the Scarecrow thoughtfully, tucking back some straw loosened by Mr. Fox's poke, "I say it maybe ten times a week, maybe more in Christmas season . . . and that would be . . ."

Mr. Fox could not bear it, this evading the subject, this eluding his argument.

"And how many have ever come home with you? This one is a marauder. A skylark. A vagrant. An impostor. All those things."

"The Boy," said the Scarecrow, motioning toward the house, "he's a good boy."

"And what makes you think so? I say he's a marauder."

It was the first time the poor Scarecrow had had a chance to describe such an exciting escapade as his race down the Straight Stretch with the Boy's life in his hands and the words poured out. ". . . He put his head asleep on my shoulder as we raced—I shudder to think of it now. So you see," said the Scarecrow logically, "he must be a good boy to have had such faith in me to go asleep on such a drive."

Mr. Fox was beaten. He *could* have demolished it all because he knew how fast (how slow) the Scarecrow had been driving down the Straight Stretch and that anybody would have to go to sleep driving with the Scarecrow, but he could not say that because it would have demolished the Scarecrow himself. Mr. Fox could not do that. He could not take the memory of that ride away from his friend even if it meant Heaven Knows What to let that boy stay around.

"And besides," said the Scarecrow definitively, "the Boy likes my porridge."

While Mr. Fox and the Scarecrow had been talking the Boy had been sitting. Sitting by the table stacked high with catalogues and magazines and newspapers, staring into the fire glowing weakly in the now bright room—day-bright warming and fire-bright burning without warming. The sun had come up over the ridge while they breakfasted. All was bright with the white light of a winter sun.

As the Boy sat he thought and knew what Mr. Fox was saying and knew he must leave. But it is hard to leave a cozy kitchen after such a breakfast, hard to leave a tiny warm house and go out alone again into the winter. It is always so hard to leave a stopping place after so short a time to rest. But the Boy knew he must.

He found an old pencil by the stove and he wrote a note to the Scarecrow on the back of a mail-order blank:

"Dear Scarecrow,

I very much thank you for your kindness to me, but I must go on and find my brother. I know you will know that I could not stay. But I did enjoy your good company and excellent breakfast.

With kindest regards and good wishes,
I am,
Samuel Hopkins Flood"

He looked at it carefully and dotted the *i*'s and crossed the *t*'s. He added:

"p.s. The porridge was very good."

He dotted the *i* again in porridge and then he stared at the fire. He went to his sheepskin coat, took something out of it, put the something on the table. He wrote again:

"p.s. I am leaving you a chestnut carved by Yours Truly into the shape of a sheep's head which (he paused and knit his brow) has been—a few times—said to be a very good carving. (He paused again and re-read and dotted and crossed and then added) By other people. But I like it, too. Or I would not give it to you."

He picked up the chestnut and fondled it and then rubbed it alongside his nose to polish it as a pipe is polished so that it gleamed brownly. His hand went to touch his one and only worldly possession—a gold ring he wore on a chain around his neck. He had worn it so long (or bathed so little) that his chest had turned a little green here and there from the gold.

Then he put on his coat and slipped out the back door and across the barn lot and behind the barn and up the old mountain road into the woods. Out of sight.

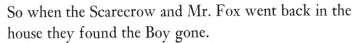

Chapter 3

So when the Scarecrow and Mr. Fox went back in the house they found the Boy gone.

"The Boy is not here," said the Scarecrow.

"Skipped," said Mr. Fox, and added ominously, "and taken Lord Knows What." Mr. Fox pushed the Scarecrow down in the chair the Boy had been sitting in and then took up his position before the fire. Having lost the battle on the lawn he was delighted that it was now self-evident the Boy was a scoundrel.

"A rascal," he said and puffed his chest. "A young

unprincipled, ungrateful scoundrel. A rogue. I knew it. The minute I heard of him, before I even saw him, I said to myself, 'He's a rogue, a rapscallion.' " Mr. Fox could feel himself getting warmer and warmer with indignation. He was also getting warmer because his tail had fallen in the fire and was beginning to smolder.

But the Scarecrow was not listening. He had found the letter and he had read the letter and great tears were rolling down his cheeks as he looked at the sheep's head. For nobody could appreciate the beautiful brown chestnut more than the Scarecrow, who loved such things.

It was so strange that as he held the gleaming brown sheep's head in his hands he could see the Boy so clearly alone going down a country road in his sheepskin coat, long-faced, long-legged, from town to town, looking for his brother.

"Fire," screamed Mr. Fox.

The Scarecrow rose like a rocket out of his chair over to the pump in the corner of the kitchen and threw water all over himself.

"No," screamed Mr. Fox, "it's not you, it's me. I'm on fire, not you."

"Well, that's good," said the Scarecrow practically. He picked up a bucket of water and walked over to where Mr. Fox was squirming and twisting trying to reach his smoking, sparkling tail.

"Now close your eyes," said the Scarecrow. When

Mr. Fox looked up the Scarecrow threw the whole bucket of water right in his face.

"It's my tail, you fool," screamed Mr. Fox.

"To be sure. I see now, of course it is." And the Scarecrow went back and got another bucket of water.

"I always felt that tail of yours would get you into trouble someday, Mr. Fox. You've let it get much too long and fluffy. Vanity, Mr. Fox!" And he threw the bucket of water over the smoldering remains of Mr. Fox's pride and joy.

"That tail has become much too important to you," the Scarecrow said, as he let fly with another bucket.

"Mean! Oh, it is mean of you to be so mean," wailed the Fox.

The Scarecrow silently handed Mr. Fox the letter to read. And then he gave him the sheep's head.

"Oh," said the Fox. "Oh, my." For even as Mr. Fox held the sheep's head in his hand he saw the Boy—the same picture that the Scarecrow had seen.

And then these two wet things sat down together on the sopping wet floor. "What have we done, Mr. Fox, what have we done? If only the Witch were here to tell us what to do about the Boy!"

"Bah!" said Mr. Fox, trying to dry himself in front of the fire—but being very careful of sparks. The Scarecrow's fireplace did not have a fire screen because he said the pit was so deep that it didn't need one and it was so huge a screen wouldn't do any good. "It's one thing we have to be thankful for—that the Witch isn't here."

There was a rush of wind outside and suddenly there was absolute stillness—complete absolute stillness.

"Now you've done it." The Fox shook his head at the Scarecrow. "You know how she hears everything. You've gone and brought her down on us."

The door opened silently. There was no sound of the latch. The door just opened. There she was. You would know she was a witch even if you had never seen her before or never been introduced because she was dressed like a witch. She simply looked like a witch.

"And what a fine miserable pair of wet wretches you two are," she declared. "And you, Mr. Fox, are the worst. The absolute worst. The Scarecrow is the wettest but you are the worst. I've been listening to you all morning. I couldn't help it. I was resting on top of the chimney. Infamous, sir, is what you are. But I have no time for you. I just stopped in to say that I am on my way to find the Boy."

The Witch spun around sharply on her metallic heel so that the long tattered skirt and shoulder cape and conical hat made her look like a fir tree. She strode out onto the big lawn beneath the great bare maples gaunt in the gray winter daylight.

"I'm coming with you," said the Scarecrow.

"And how do you suppose you can come with me? I hope you don't think I'm going to look for this precious boy of yours on foot. Really, Scarecrow!" The Witch walked to the fence where she had left her broomstick and swirled her cape around her shoulder.

"And with all the things I have to do at home." She shook her head. The Witch was always complaining about the things she had to do at home. The Scarecrow had never been able to understand if you were a witch —a real capable, sound, sensible witch like this witch —how you could have any problems getting done when you could do anything so fast.

"But I *must* come with you," pleaded the Scarecrow. "I'll ride behind and . . . and I promise you I won't fall off. I know what I'll do . . . I'll close my eyes. You drive. And I'll close my eyes and won't say a word."

"Impossible."

"Please."

The Witch put her broom between her legs and adjusted her skirts. It was a point with her to look graceful on her broomstick. There was so much sloppy flying these days. When she flew she liked her skirts to flow out like birds' wings. Also she crisscrossed her ankles so that her long toes pointed away from each other. They mustn't dangle.

"Please. I beg you."

"No. It's bad for the balance."

The Scarecrow looked so pitiful and forlorn that she could not resist and she showed him how to get on. Beaming, he sat behind her. Beaming, he put his hands around her waist.

"My, you are bony," he observed. He added hastily, "Oh, I mean I envy you to be so bony as that. I am so squashy, you know . . . I hate being squashy."

The Witch's cape had slipped, and now she flung it sharply around so as to snap it right in Mr. Scarecrow's face. Mr. Fox came running out of the house as the broomstick started to move.

"Wait for me! Wait for me!"

"Let us go," said the Scarecrow calmly and closed his eyes.

Gently, ever so gently. Like a swan. The Scarecrow felt all weight leave. He had never felt so free. It was intoxicating. It wasn't scary at all.

"Let me come, too. Wait for me." The Scarecrow could hear Mr. Fox calling, fainter now, and running along beneath them, now tiny, beating his chest vainly. The Scarecrow hated heights but he could not resist peeking at this. To see Mr. Fox running along beneath them. So small. So furious. Then he started to pitch sideways and he closed his eyes tight.

He squeezed the Witch so tight she screamed and giggled. She thought he was hugging her.

"Oh, Scarecrow, really! At a moment like this. Now do be yourself."

But then it was all right. The Scarecrow knew that he was in the clear—he had won his wings. Over the Witch's shoulder he could see the long running blue mountains of the Appalachians stretching as far as he could see. Gray and dark, sleeping beneath the dark winter sky. He could see beneath him the unbelievable neatness of meadows etched by gray rail fences and dotted with neat round haystacks each fenced with its own gray rail. The haystacks, each with its fence and hay pole rising like a mast, were an armada sailing down the valley.

The Scarecrow had never seen such a sight. He had lived in this country, this magic country, all his life—and he had walked the hills in all the seasons of the year to see his sheep and he had walked the roads and had gone over every inch of meadow late in the evening on a haymaking day to catch the last slips of hay on the tines of his fork. But he had never seen this country. Not like this, rolling all the way away. To the windy corners of the world, to the blue horizon. Almost now it was as if he were still down there on the land with the sheep where they roamed, head down, over the pasture for the last of summer's sprigs. Little white balls they were against the soft of the brown hill. How often can you see where you belong?

It had been a wonderful ride. He would not have missed it for the world, but he was ready to go down. Suddenly the Scarecrow understood why the Witch was petulant sometimes. Dissatisfied. She spent too much time on this broom flying over land that didn't belong to her and where she didn't belong. Irresponsible. Chasing rainbows, chasing butterflies, chasing sunsets. Pretending she could be a creature on the wing. Witch can't help it if she seems flighty sometimes, thought the Scarecrow.

They were swooping lower now, following the brown rutted road up the mountain to the Harris place. Suddenly the Scarecrow saw the Boy sitting by the side of the road. He took one hand from around the Witch to point. When she turned to look he lost his balance. Suddenly he was holding onto the broomstick with only one hand, which might have been all right except for the way he was doing it. He was hanging on one end of the broomstick with one hand . . . It was dreadful. He thought his arm would break. It was certainly getting longer every minute.

The Witch was losing control. She couldn't keep the broomstick level with the Scarecrow hanging down like that from the other end.

They were sinking. The Scarecrow could see the mountain coming up. There was a splintery woody crash. They were hung up in the upper branches of a very tall oak.

Someone had told the Scarecrow a long time ago that the thing to do at a moment like this was to be matter of fact. "We are in the upper branches of a tall oak tree," he said. It made him so happy that he could hear his own voice. It was a strong indication that he was still alive.

"What did you think it was—a field of poppies? Why I ought to . . . (she tried for her broomstick but it was out of reach). Boy! Come here, Boy! (They had both almost forgotten about him but there he was, freckle-faced, yellow hair tangled and long face grinning up at them.) You come and take me out of this oak tree this instant!"

Chapter 4

Somehow the Boy climbed the tree and disentangled the Witch and her broom. The Scarecrow was more difficult. He was all tangled in the branches. But the Scarecrow suffered silently. He did not want to call his presence too forcefully to the mind of the Witch. In fact he wished that he wasn't even there. He was afraid of thinking that too loud for fear that the Witch would grant his wish and he might not be there—in fact might not be anywheres at all—which was difficult to imagine but certainly awful to think about.

Fortunately for the Scarecrow the Witch was much too busy muttering as she tried to set herself and her broom to rights.

"And on a day like this, too, wouldn't you know (she struggled with the stick part of the broom) as if (she bent it sharply) as if (she bent it hard) I didn't have enough to do (something snapped). Now it never will fly again. I know it. And I've had it for years."

The main problem was the broom part of the broom. The ends were all going off in different directions. But by twisting here and bending there she finally succeeded in sort of getting it back into some sort of shape. Finally she was satisfied.

"Now Boy," she said, "come here. I want to get a good look at you."

"Yes," she said, "somebody in town said you were familiar and you are." She reached in her pocket and took out a large glasses case and out of the large glasses case she took a small pair of spectacles which she fitted carefully over her ears so that they sat on the tip of her long nose. The most interesting thing was that there was no glass in the spectacles.

"Of course," she said, "it's obvious now. And your name?"

"Samuel Hopkins Flood."

"No," said the Witch, "but I haven't time to talk now." She mounted her broomstick and was about to shove off.

"But," said the Scarecrow rushing up, unable to contain himself, "what do you mean, 'No'?"

The Witch shook her head impatiently. "No, no, I don't mean Yes if I say No, do I? The Boy's name is not Samuel (she sputtered) well whatever he said it was it isn't."

"But . . . but," said the Scarecrow.

"But," said the Witch, "I must go." Mounted on her broomstick, she slowly rose, wobbled, swooped, now rose again trying to learn the touch of the new twists and bends in her old broom, gained speed, lost it, dropped. Then up she went and finally wobbled slowly off into the distance, her torn skirt flying blackly, bravely behind her.

"You better come home with me, Boy," said the Scarecrow, and although it was only an expression, this time the Scarecrow meant it, and he took the Boy by the hand so that there could be no misunderstanding.

It was almost night when the two of them walked up through the orchard, beneath the bare gray-black branches, and came in sight of the tiny house beneath the great trees.

"But it's lighted," said the Scarecrow. "Oh, dear, someone is in my house."

"Maybe it's Mr. Fox," said the Boy, glad to be back. "Maybe Mr. Fox is in there."

"He wouldn't stay around with his tail in that condition."

"And besides he doesn't like me."

"And besides he's much too vain. Shhh . . . we'll creep up and we—maybe you—can surprise our mysterious visitor."

The Scarecrow's idea of creeping up was to get down on his knees and creep up. With the Boy creeping behind him very close. The Scarecrow dragged himself along the ground like a crocodile and kept kicking the Boy to make sure he was there. Fortunately his feet, being made of straw, were quite soft and squashy.

Thus these two crept up to the house. They crept around the house. They crept foot by foot, inch by inch, toe by toe. Finally the Boy stopped creeping to wait for the Scarecrow to make a suggestion. The Scarecrow kicked him again. They crept around the house again. As they started around a third time the Boy whispered, "I'm going to peek in the window."

"Not on your life," said the Scarecrow, "or mine either. We'll let him make the first mistake."

They crept around the house again.

"This is the fourth time," said the Boy.

The Scarecrow kicked him.

The Boy's knees were beginning to hurt. "Just one peek?"

"Not when we have him on the run," said the Scarecrow, and began to creep around the house again.

"Stop! Listen!" whispered the Boy. "I hear something strange going on in there."

They listened.

There was a scraping sound, then a whirring flopping sound, then sort of a plop, then a scraping sound, then a whirring flopping sound, then sort of a plop, then . . .

"I don't hear a thing," said the Scarecrow, getting closer to the Boy.

"Now, Scarecrow, be sensible."

"It's the wind."

They had happened to stop right by the door. And suddenly . . . the door flew open. The light from the house flooded out.

With remarkable presence of mind the Scarecrow pushed the Boy's head into the ground and put his own head right down next to him.

"Don't look up," said the Scarecrow. "Don't let him know we're here. Just be invisible."

Nothing happened. And then—they sensed a figure in the doorway—the Devil himself!

"Will you two idiots come in before the whole house gets cold and the pancakes ruined!" And there was Mr. Fox in the most magnificent red apron and chef's hat standing in the doorway.

"Well, Fox!" huffed the Scarecrow, getting up shaking himself, "why didn't you say it was you?"

"Is that all you have to say for yourself?" said Fox.

"You can thank your lucky stars, Fox. In another minute the Boy probably would not have been able to restrain me. I'd have burst in and had it out. Oh, Mr. Fox (rushing up and hugging him) I probably would have killed you in cold blood before I knew who it was . . . Oh, you wonderful Fox (coming into the house) what have you done?"

There was the table heaped with milk and syrup and butter and in the center a plate of steaming brown pancakes, maybe a foot high.

Mr. Fox took charge. "Now Boy, you sit here." And the Boy did. Mr. Fox forked out the crisp brown pancakes and the butter melted on them and the syrup poured out dark brown and sweet.

They ate.

Mr. Fox stood in front of the burnished black cookstove in his red apron and big puffy hat and flopped pancakes—scraped and flipped them, caught them neatly and added to the dwindling pile in the center of the table until the Boy began to moan and the Scarecrow's corn-tassel forelock began to turn green and the Boy looked a shade less so but was getting there.

They groaned. They stared into the fire and groaned some more.

"Thank you, Mr. Fox," said the Boy. "They were the greatest. They were great pancakes."

"I've never had better, here or abroad," said the Scarecrow.

"I can see you have judgment, Boy," said the Fox. "The secret of a pancake is how it is flopped."

"Flipped," said the Scarecrow.

"If you will," said the Fox magnanimously. "But the important thing is that you're back, Boy."

"But did you know, Mr. Fox, that the Boy's name is not Samuel Hopkins Flood?" The Scarecrow wanted to be the first to tell.

"It's not?"

"The Witch told us."

It must be said for Mr. Fox that while he might be overly suspicious he was—once he felt he could trust, which was almost never—he was overly trusting.

"Well, then that must be so. After all, Boy, between us, sometimes all of us use a nom de plume, eh? Or a nom de guerre, eh?"

"The facts are," said the Boy, "the Witch is right. Samuel Hopkins Flood is not my real name, but it is the only name I have."

"That explains it," said the Scarecrow.

"There is nothing more to be said," offered the Fox generously.

"Consider the matter closed," said the Scarecrow.

"Certainly," said Mr. Fox.

"We would be the last to pry, my boy," said the Scarecrow.

"What you have done you have done," said the Fox in his deepest Sunday voice.

"No, you don't understand," said the Boy. "You see the town where I was born was washed away in the great Ohio River flood." And he told his story:

He had, as a baby in that flood, floated down the Ohio River in a cradle and been washed ashore. The couple who had found him were named Hopkins and it happened on St. Samuel's Day and so he had been named for the way it happened—Samuel Hopkins Flood.

This couple had raised him with their children after no one had come for him. They had even advertised about having found an extra baby in the Ohio River. There had been nothing to mark the Boy except a man's ring on a chain about his neck. It was supposed that the father had done this to somehow give the baby an identification.

The Boy might have stayed with the Hopkinses. But they had wanted to move west. The Boy felt that somehow his future lay in the great mountains to the east that rise from the Ohio River and stretch to the Shenandoah.

He told people, if they asked, he was looking for his brother. He had found it was a good reason. People seemed to understand it. You can't say, if you're a boy, as you go down a lonely mountain road, that you don't know where you're going, that you're trying to find out where you came from and who you are. That you are seeking warmth and strength or love or whatever.

But you can say you're looking for your brother and people don't think you're crazy.

If you asked the Boy how he happened to come here, to this land on top of the world, he would have just said that the roads led him here. He knew he was right for he had met a strange old woman along the road. She had called him The Boy with the Green Chest and she had told him his fortune:

When a man who can't hear
Hears you
When a man who can't see
Sees you
When a man who can't walk
Comes to you
Then the man who can't talk
Will tell you.

Chapter 5

The Boy stayed with the Scarecrow that late winter.
Life fell into place. In winter on a small farm, one like
the Scarecrow's hilly cove, like all the other mountain
hollows each with a lone house around a crooked bend
in the road, you spend your time feeding the animals,
staying warm, eating and sleeping.

It is good to be alive in the winter. There is the cold
chilling dash from bed to the warm kitchen where you
can get dressed in front of a hot fire (if the Scarecrow
has gotten up first to make it). Then a glorious hot

breakfast of porridge and brown sugar and apple butter rich with the taste of Smokehouse and Maiden Blush and late summer's golden Greenings. Then while you're still warm, out to the barn where the cow wants milking. The milk streams warm and sweet into the pail, the cow is happy, and the hay drips down like moss and tickles the nose like lavender.

Wood to bring in. The sheep to be fed. The chickens to tend. The pigs. The horse is hungry too, and the barn wants cleaning.

And then there were trips to the Mail Box. The Scarecrow always went on Thursday. It was when the *Mountain Gazette* came. If the Scarecrow had been in town the week before there would be a paragraph in the "From Out of Town" column: "All were pleased to see the Scarecrow visiting in town on Tuesday. He bought a new thermometer. Did the last cold wave break the old one? Ha-Ha."

And then there is always a little time to do nothing —to sit on a fence and look down the valley, to watch the smoke come out of the chimney, swirl and disappear.

Some days are so nearly the same, you have certainly done that day before, but other days are different and one small thing leads to a whole lot of other things. Like the afternoon the milk cow was missing. The one that was heavy with calf.

A panel of fence was down where she had wandered

off. It was one of those strange warm foggy days in winter that always come and always surprise you, with the air so soft and the ground spongy instead of hard and velvety green-gold instead of withered like old parchment. These days always confuse you by making everything smell and touch like spring even in the middle of winter.

The Boy followed her tracks up the hill into the woods along the little path beneath the bare dogwood and past the green myrtle. Past the thickets of mountain laurel. The way took the Boy farther than he had ever been and just when he thought he must be at the edge of the property he came to the line fence. Here was a tree down across the fence and the cow most probably gone across between two big old rusted NO–TRESPASSING signs.

Then suddenly the trail led out of the woods onto a small rise and here was a new valley stretching as far as he could see—low rolling hills, once-rich pasture going to brush, rough fields sprouting clumps of locust, wiry, tall, and old brown stands of briar and fallen trees and coarse grass and ruddy sage that stood almost as tall as the Boy. Parts of old rail fences stood here and there. A land that had been cleared was going back to the forest, returning to the forest that some man had cleared for his sons, had fenced for a kingdom, and had given up on. It was not the big-treed forest it had been. Now it was only a scrubby briary dirty piece of ground that belonged neither to man nor to the forest.

The Boy stood for an instant studying the place. He knew that it meant something—this half-wilderness. But he had to find the cow. It was easy to follow her path through the heavy grass. Every once in a while he stopped to listen for her bell. The Boy quickened his pace now because he knew that cows, if they could, sometimes went a long way off to calve and if this was what she had done it would be a long ways to come back with a new calf that didn't walk very fast and would have to be carried.

He was trying to find his way around a briar patch when he heard someone call him.

"Boy, where do you think you're going?" There was a very tall old man in a great caped coat and a long walking stick.

"I'm looking for our cow, sir. I think she's gone off to drop a calf."

"She don't belong here, Boy. I don't allow cows or boys on this property."

"No, sir." But the Boy did not move.

"Well?" said the Old Man.

The Boy stood his ground and stared back.

Finally it was the Old Man who broke the silence, "Begone!"

"Yessir." The Boy barked it out and turned and went on his way after the cow.

"Boy!" the Old Man called. "I said to get off this property."

"I will—after I find my cow."

"The cow be damned. I'll have her sent back."

The Boy shook his head. "The fence was down, the line fence where a tree's come down on it, and we have to get our own stock back because it was our tree."

"And where did you learn that?"

"It's the law, sir."

The Old Man nodded. "And do you know how big this property is?" He held out his cane and made an arc around him as if to take in all the land in sight. "I'll tell you. It's over ten thousand acres and it's wide open. There's not a fence standing in it and that cow can wander so far you'll never find her."

The Boy had turned now to look over the hills.

"I expect she might go for that big sinkhole where the run comes down from the mountain. I expect I might find her there."

The Old Man came up close to the Boy now. "So you know this property, do you? So you've made a habit of coming over here. You've probably had your damned cow here all winter eating her head off. Well, let me tell you, Boy, this grass is not for your cow or any animal to eat. Nothing is going to eat here. This land is going back to brush and someday no one will ever know there was a farm here. That's the way I want it and that's the way it's going to be. You hear? "

The Boy had not meant to say what he did but the words had simply come out about that big sinkhole. He felt he had been here before. He *knew* what was over that hill. He knew it was a hiding place a cow might go to drop a calf.

"No, sir," he said, doubting himself some. "But I just figured there was a big sinkhole—I could see it sort of. But I have never seen it."

"You lie, Boy. You lie."

The Boy now came very close to the Old Man and looked up at him. "I tell no lies, Old Man—and not to one like you."

The Old Man colored and spoke sharp.

"You talk strange but you bluff well, Boy, and I tell you now to get off my property or I'll flail you within an inch of your life." He raised his cane.

The Boy moved out of his reach. "No, Old Man, and you can't catch me. And now I'm going to get my damned cow." He ran over the hill toward the big sinkhole. The cow was just struggling now to calve. The boy sat down on his haunches on the slope of the sinkhole to watch—not wanting to disturb her if all went well. She had found her resting place, her hiding place for the struggle of birth.

The cow strained. She breathed hard. She strained more. Then she stood up and circled again to make her bed. But when she lay down again and strained again it was not coming right.

The Old Man had come up behind the Boy finally and stood there silently. The Boy sat very still watching, studying. Finally, when it seemed the moment of agony could be held back no longer, the cow seemed straining so, in such pain, he went down to her. Wanting to help her even if he did not know how.

The Old Man came slowly down, too. He wanted these creatures off his property. He wanted no life here. He wanted no life to be born here. He wanted the brush to come. But this was birth and there is nothing to be done for that. Here was this boy wanting to help and not knowing how.

"Boy, you see the foot of the calf is caught. Straighten it. Pull it forward. When you catch it don't lose it for the cow may give you but one chance and it's a slippery thing, slippery beyond anything you know."

The Boy did what the Old Man said. Never looking up at all. Working cool and efficient to make the leg come free. And it was slippery beyond anything he knew but the leg came free. The next time the cow strained the calf came out all smooth and slick and steamy and lay panting on the ground.

The Boy saw to it that its throat was clear and then he stood up.

"How did you know to do that?" asked the Old Man.

The Boy shook his head. "Must be what you told me to do gave me the idea of what to do next."

"Well done," said the Old Man. Impressed.

The Boy and the Old Man sat on the side of the sinkhole and watched the newborn calf come to life —or rather watched the ebb and flow of Life as it came to the little calf. It came gently, fluttering a tiny awakening ear, as a summer's breeze stirs a blossom. It came achingly, pulling at the hooves and haunches and dragging the heavy head and making it jerk. It came harshly with the rough tongue of the mother who licked it clean so that the white fur stood out silky and clean. Whiter than it ever would be again. The calf struggled to get up but the mother was not through fussing with it yet. Finally it charged to its feet and stood there triumphantly on all four of them, wobbled, and then, after all that effort, fell down again beneath the off-balancing impact of a final lick.

The next time the baby calf struggled to its feet it walked. It walked all wobbly with its head down—but thrust forward, muzzle raised hungrily searching the sky.

Now it staggered between the cow's legs, knocked into one and collapsed. The sky that it was searching for was lost, but only for a moment and the calf was back up again, lurching about. The mother stood still now. Before, when the calf had careened through her legs, she had stepped about very delicately as if her hooves had mysterious diviners to detect the whereabouts of her offspring—a curious stately ladylike stepping-in-and-out.

Now she just stood while the calf did its dance. A dance which it had never danced before but which it somehow remembered—because every newborn calf knows this dance. The cow stood still while the calf bumbled around, in its awkwardness yet full of grace, light on its feet as a feather, looking for it knew not what, poking with cold nose at this strange big beast, circling again, knowing that this was the thing to do, to poke and bump, and then at last a sudden something soft and wonder-of-wonders something warm. Warm to drink. Warm enough to drown in. The calf guzzled. He drank so much he fell down again. He would have gotten up, he could have gotten up, you know, but it had been a long day, perhaps the longest day he remembered. He was very sleepy.

Chapter 6

The Boy was weary. Somehow the cow and calf
must be gotten back. While the calf snoozed the Boy
and the Old Man spoke no words but the Boy stared
about him and the Old Man stared downwards.

When he started out home the Boy tried carrying
the calf, which had exhausted itself with its dancing.
This didn't work very well because the cow kept
going back to where she had last seen the calf. Besides
it was quite a heavy calf, or it seemed to grow so. The

Old Man was following now on horseback and whenever they stopped he stopped.

A mist had fallen now as the winter evening came on and pulled the sun low in the sky. It filled the hollows and the sinkholes. The drops stood out like stars stuck on the bare brown of the briars. Now, not livened by the fading sun, the paling woods lost the pink-brown glow of a winter afternoon and the late clinging curly red oak leaves looked like millions of little bats waiting for the dark. Two lone whippoorwills shouted raucously to each other, one near, one far. The cow's bell rang out unsymmetrically as she nervously looked for her calf which was tucked in the Boy's arms where he sat on a huge fallen tree.

The Boy panted tiredly. The calf rested its chin on his arm and was comforted and looked out at the new world beneath long soft gentle clean white lashes that flickered at the slightest movement. The calf sneezed and straightaway the cow came running up, shaking her bell like an old woman.

Finally the Old Man trotted up alongside the Boy. He said nothing. The Old Man stretched down one arm and the Boy said nothing but handed up the calf to the Old Man who took it in his lap and held it with both arms in a cradle and with his knees guiding the horse. They made good time now. The Old Man leading the way. The calf tucked quietly in his arms. The Boy driving the cow.

She protested. Why couldn't she be alone? She wanted to go back to the sinkhole where her calf was. She knew it was still back there. She must go back to it. She turned suddenly and knocked the Boy off his feet. But she was not quite quick enough. He caught her by the tail. He held her. The Old Man rode back. He stopped close by the cow so that she could see the calf. He let her lick for a moment for identification. There was no doubt that the calf she had left in the sinkhole was now here. She stayed very close now.

They kept on going until the barn came into sight. The Boy took the calf from the Old Man.

"You better come home with me," the Old Man said as he turned the horse's head with a smooth sweep of his hands, thin and blue-veined hands but strong but not the way they once were.

"You better come home with me, Boy," he repeated.

And he was gone before the Boy could say a word. When he shouted after him, "Thank you. Good night, sir," the Old Man neither turned nor looked back but went straight up the wooded hill into the heart of the forest.

The cow now made as if to go back again to the sinkhole. The Boy put the calf down, as close to its mother's nose as possible. At first the mother didn't see it at all and the Boy had a moment of terror that she would run off again. Then she saw it. She saw her wonderful white clean calf. She came running to it with heels high and the bell swinging widely, sweetly, to find this tiny thing she thought she'd lost. She gave it an extra lick under the chin and knocked it down.

"You silly cow. Oh, you silly, silly cow!" The Boy sat down on his haunches, and then flopped onto his back and lay there all stretched out staring up at the sky.

The Boy never mentioned his visit with the Old Man to anyone. Not to the Scarecrow, or Mr. Fox, or to the Witch. If you had asked him he would not have known why except that he wanted to keep it to himself—perhaps because it was not yet enough to tell. It was not yet finished.

He had tried to find out about the Old Man. His name was Wing. He owned this farm next to the Scarecrow. He owned another large farm at the other end of the county. That was where he lived now. He had lived here at the place where the Boy had seen him. That was before the Old Man's son had left. It seems that the Old Man and his son had parted over the son's choice of wife. The son who would have inherited his father's world had left. Never been heard of again so far as anybody knew. Or cared. People who moved away from this mountain world didn't count. But the Old Man had cared. He lived alone and unapproachable.

Sometimes on Saturday night the Boy saw the Old Man in town riding down Main Street, very straight upon his horse, in his big cape. Like a king, the Boy thought. Except there are no kings in our country riding at the head of great glorious armies. In our country an old man's armies are his memories and he must live and relive them until he dies. This was an old king. He still had his ten thousand acres and he owned a mountain at the other end of the county, but he was riding back from defeat. At some time in his life he had lost a battle, a very big battle. He had come back alive but the heart was dead, and the people who didn't count still thought of him as a king and got out of his way when he came down Main Street on Saturday night.

There is no chance to fight the battle again for a very old man and he can only try to sit a little extra straight in the saddle as he rides along without any battle to go to and even though the people who don't count are the only ones to see.

Once when the Boy was standing on the steps of Mr. Nagle's store he saw the Old Man come down Main Street, looking neither to the right nor left, and then he looked over to where the Boy was standing in faded blue jeans and sheepskin coat and his hair very blond beneath the light overhead coming out the door. Ever, ever so gently, slowly, courtly as a king, the Old Man raised one gloved hand in a half-salute. The Boy was caught so entranced he did nothing, that is, nothing outside but inside he felt his heart give an extra thump and come up into his throat beating.

That was the night on the way home when the Scarecrow announced it was to snow. That it was to be the Big Snow—the one that came at the end of every winter. The Scarecrow insisted. There are times you know. You can feel it in the gray sky hanging low and smell it in the night air, you can hear it in the soft wind that had begun to blow and even the old horse tonight wanted to get home.

The Boy did not feel it. Nor smell it nor hear it . . . the great snow closing in upon them like an avalanche, a soft mysterious white mountain rising, a thick white dull heavy fog falling. Even as they went down the black Straight Stretch and the first great flakes were dropping softly, silencing the world, muffling it in a thousand million softly dropping white flakes he still saw in the mind's eye, in the heart's leap he still felt, the Old Man's salute. Which he had not returned.

Chapter 7

The next morning the world was white. The world, the whole world was white except for streaks of wet black and herringbone gray. The road was gone. There was only an expanse of whiteness, a blanket of smooth, un-footprinted, un-stepped-in whiteness. Suddenly this little attic had become the top of an island. There was no land to be seen—the stumps were gone, even the fences. The hills were marshmallow smooth. Every rough edge in the world was gone.

Now there in the distance was something moving

. . . bobbing up and down, disappearing but still coming on . . . something red, something furry, something in a hurry, something like Mr. Fox!

The Boy rushed to get downstairs and into his clothes at the same time.

"Scarecrow, Mr. Fox is coming!"

"Of course." Scarecrow was sitting at the kitchen table sorting out buttons.

"Of course? Why do you say, 'Of course'?" The Boy was dressed now. It doesn't take a boy long to dress.

All the Boy ate were mouthfuls. "Of course?" he said between mouthfuls.

"Oh these buttons!" the Scarecrow said, ignoring the question. "I get so mixed up."

"What are you going to do with the buttons on the first day of the Big Snow? You must be going to sew them on something?"

"Sew them on, did you say, *sew* them on? Sometimes, Boy—oh, thank heavens, there is Mr. Fox. He'll have something sensible to say—I hope."

Mr. Fox came in looking very wintry—with icicles on his eyebrows and whiskers—and acting very busily businesslike.

"Well, you're both ready—I hope. If you knew how long it took me to get here." He looked around. He looked at the buttons closely. "I like these two." He picked out two shiny bright blue ones.

"I did, too," said the Scarecrow. "But you know how he is."

"I know," said Mr. Fox. "I do know. Sometimes I think we make a mistake in picking the buttons for how they look to us and not for how they look."

"You're dead right," said Mr. Scarecrow.

"You're confusing me," said the Boy.

"You have the cane," asked Mr. Fox, "and the hat?"

"Yes, and the pipe. I'm sure we've forgotten something. Oh yes, the other buttons. I'll take the box and let him pick . . . he'll like to do that."

"Well done," said the Fox. "You're always so organized. Here we go. I suppose the Witch will be there already. If she's not grounded—eh! Boy, not grounded? Good, eh? Come along."

"Where?" asked the Boy sensibly.

"Don't pay any attention to him," said the Scarecrow. "He's been acting like that all morning."

"Acting like what?" said the Boy, putting on his sheepskin coat and lacing his boots.

"Acting stupid, Boy. Acting ignorant," said Mr. Fox. "After all, it is the Big Snow that ends the winter."

Mr. Fox took the cane, they gave the Boy the hat (a magnificent brown derby) and Mr. Scarecrow took the button box and the pipe.

They stepped out into the snow and the Scarecrow disappeared, red scarf and all.

"The buttons," he screamed as he went down under. They found the buttons—that came first. Then they found the Scarecrow. He was so furious he couldn't speak. He hated to get snow down inside of himself.

"Won't *he* love this weather," said the Fox to himself.

The Boy did not make the mistake of asking "Who?" this time. Who would want to be called stupid twice so early in the morning? He just followed along. Mr. Fox led the way. Which was good because his great red tail (its bushiness fully recovered) made such a lovely path. They went up through the barn meadow. And over the fence gate without needing to open it. It was very grand to walk right over the top of the fence.

They started up the Peach Tree Hill where the small trees stood out wet black against the gray sky and against the gray-white porpoiselike hill. It was quiet. So quiet that once they stopped, the three of them on the side of the hill, listening—just for some sound, some wind, some bird, but it was absolutely snow-whitely still.

They were almost at the top when they first saw it—on top of the Peach Tree Hill was a great white figure.

"There he is," said the Scarecrow.

"Of course he is," said an impatient voice. It was the Witch, hopskipping along on her broom. "I thought you would never get here. I've been talking to him for an hour. I might just as well have been talking to myself because you had all the stuff."

The figure, the great white figure was a Snowman —the Snowman—a big fat Snowman with one hand outstretched.

"All right," said the Witch.

"I always do it," said the Scarecrow defensively.

"That's why I should do it," said Mr. Fox.

"Let the Boy do it," said the Scarecrow.

"Yes, yes, let the Boy do it," said the Witch and Mr. Fox together. "Let the Boy do it."

They gave the Boy the hat and he put it on the Snowman. They gave the Boy the pipe and he put it in the Snowman's mouth.

"Now," said the Scarecrow, "here are the eyes for the Snowman to see."

The Boy took the blue buttons very carefully and he put one eye in here, and he put the other eye— there.

"And now you can see, Snowman."

"And now I can see, Boy," said the Snowman. "And I thank you, all my friends, for coming here today. And Boy, I am most glad to see you back!"

Chapter 8

"The buttons! The buttons!" shouted the Scarecrow.

"Yes, of course," shouted the Fox. "The buttons. We have a box this year. To pick from."

The Snowman examined the box carefully. "That one," he would say. "Oh, I do like that one. No, not that one, it doesn't do anything for me—do you think? Big ones, I want big ones." Now the Snowman was complete.

Almost. The Boy had been standing very quiet. Now he snatched the Scarecrow's red scarf and tossed it up so it landed just perfectly around the Snowman's neck.

"And now," said the Snowman, "you must tell me the news." It bothered the Boy the way the Snowman talked because there was no movement, no emotion. Nothing except the voice which came out deep from the inside of the Snowman. And it was frightening to imagine how anchored down it must feel. Sort of like a man in a cast—in a great white plaster cast that covers all of him except you know that there is a being, a person, a life down in the center of all this cold whiteness.

"And the date, Mr. Fox—is it early or is it late this year?"

"It's the sixteenth day of March, Snowman."

"The sixteenth? That's good, I think. Wouldn't you say, Witch, that it's good?"

"I would have to agree with that. It's certainly earlier than sometimes."

"Earlier than the twentieth," said the Scarecrow helpfully.

"Earlier than the seventeenth," said Mr. Fox.

"Ha, ha . . . that's very good, Mr. Fox. . . ." Laughter rolled out of the Snowman. Great blobs of snow shook off him into Mr. Fox's face. In fact, Mr. Fox's spectacles were blown off.

"Ha, ha!" said Scarecrow, who did not help Fox look for them. "Now perhaps you know how I felt with the buttons."

The Boy felt awkward and un-at-home with the Snowman and even strange with his friends, who he sensed were not at ease. They were somehow too eager to please, to pamper the Snowman. As if, you might say, the Snowman were an invalid, or an aged relation paying a once-a-year visit.

"You see, Boy," said the Snowman, talking to the Boy as if he had always known him and as if he read his thoughts, "it is important to me what the date is. Because I come alive on the first day of the last snow of the year. I am alive until it melts and if the last snow is early sometimes I am here for quite a while. Sometimes if the last snow is late I am not here very long at all."

"But you come every year," said the Scarecrow impatiently. "Every year you come." Philosophizing always made him nervous and impatient.

"And every year the three of you come," said the Snowman, puffing on his pipe.

"He's getting very good at that," said the Fox. "The first year he couldn't make it work at all."

"And every year now the four of you will come," went on the Snowman. "How long have you been doing this?"

"Ever since we found the hat, and the cane, and the pipe, and the buttons one spring here on the Peach Tree Hill," said the Witch.

"And you, Boy," said the Snowman, "the Witch has been telling me about you."

The Boy wondered whether that was good or bad. "I come from over the mountain."

"To be sure. To be sure. And now while there is still time you must tell me the news."

And the three of them—the Scarecrow, the Witch, and Mr. Fox—told him. Told him of the barns that had burned, the people that had died, the drought—the worst since '31—and the floods and the tornadoes, the people that had been married and the babies that had been born—all the news of the year that had happened. And Scarecrow may have told some that didn't happen. What amazed them all was that in such a dull year so many things had happened worth telling.

At the end of the news the Snowman said nothing about all that had happened but he did say, "You have no idea what it is like to stand here again at the top of the world and look down this hollow, down this white hollow, toward the mountains. Each time it is like a new time." He seemed to shudder and flakes of snow came off. "But I should like to see the hollow in spring or summer too, and you must tell me again about those colors you have in the fall."

All of them stared with him down the white slope over the small house with the wisps of smoke curling up and beyond to the blue mountains—blue any time of year.

They lingered like that.

Finally, "Well," said the Witch briskly, "I should be

off. There is so much to do this time of year. I have left my kitchen in a state of rather confusion." She mounted. "You better come home with me." And then she was gone. Into the clouds, on to the horizon, the Witch of the Blue Mountains.

"We should be going, too," said the Scarecrow.

"It was nice to meet you," said the Boy. "I never knew. They never told me."

"You will come back."

"Yes, yes, I will come back," said the Boy.

The three of them went slowly down the hill toward the Scarecrow's house. Nobody said a word. Nobody said a single word until they were back in front of the fire with hot cider.

"It's too bad," said Mr. Fox. "It's a sad case."

"I thought he looked very well," said the Scarecrow glumly.

"Yes, he did. He certainly did," said the Fox in despair.

"He seems very sad," said the Boy.

"It's the melting." The Scarecrow shook his head. "You see, it's the melting."

"But not yet," said the Boy.

"Oh, no, not now, but you see he knows he can't last long. Spring always comes."

"It's a very sad case." The Fox tried to cover up his emotion by being pontifical. "He lasts such a little time."

"But you'd think he would be happy now—when he is here."

"You'd think so—it's depressing, I agree," said the Scarecrow. "You know how it is, Boy, Mr. Fox and I, we both look forward to it so—I want so much to get up there first thing when the last snow falls, and then, and then it's just so depressing."

"Life," said Mr. Fox.

"Melting," said the Scarecrow. "Can you imagine yourself melting, Mr. Fox?"

"With your eyes dropping out," said Mr. Fox.

"It makes you wonder," said the Scarecrow.

"It certainly does," said Mr. Fox.

The Boy went up every day after that to talk with the Snowman. He hunkered down on his heels, sitting on them so that the back of him did not touch the snow. It was comfortable that way. It was the way he always sat outside.

"But don't you expect," the Boy said, looking up at the Snowman, "that someday you might walk?"

"Impossible, Boy, impossible. I was not made to walk. And I can't walk. I don't even really want to walk. This is where I belong. Everybody, Boy, belongs somewhere. You'll learn that some day. I'm really very lucky. To know where I belong. To be where I belong."

"Everybody?"

"Everybody."

"How about the Witch?"

"That's her trouble. She refuses to belong anywhere."

"And where do I belong? Tell me, Snowman. I want to know. It's easy for you, or the Scarecrow. You know, but I don't."

"You belong here, Boy, right here."

"You mean right here, on the Peach Tree Hill? All alone on top of the Peach Tree Hill? That's where I belong?" The Boy laughed and laughed.

"You're not alone. You're with me. I don't waste breath for your amusement, Boy. I mean here. In this hollow, in this country on top of the world, cut off from all the rest of the world by the Blue Mountains. This is where you belong, Boy."

"Sometimes I think you're right, Snowman. Sometimes it's as if I have been here before. Sometimes I know what lies over a hill I've never been over. But that's only sometimes. Other times I think I have to move on and find something else."

"You stay right here, Boy."

"I will . . . as long as . . ."

"As long as what, Boy?"

"As long as you're here, Snowman. I'll stay here at least until then."

"I thought that's what you meant."

"You don't mind my saying that—do you, Snowman? I mean I know one shouldn't talk about such things, but I thought that you and I—we only talk about important things."

"Quite true," sighed the Snowman. "No, I don't think I do mind. That's because you are you and I am I. You see, I live up here, way up here each year in the snow and I have my mountains and my sky. And the wind. I have the wind. I have the sounds. Sometimes a tree falls on the mountain in the middle of a silent night with a great tearing echoing crash. And then all of a sudden there is absolute silence again." The Snowman paused, lost in thought.

"So I have these things. These mountains. Where was I?"

"You were talking about important things."

"That's it. I was talking about talking about important things. And my point is I live all the time with important things—as you call them—and so naturally I talk about them."

"And how come you know I belong here?"

"Because I know who made me, Boy. That's how I know. It happened a long time ago. I do know who you are—except that there's one part of the story I can't quite remember. The proof. You see there is a way you can prove who you are. That's the part I've forgotten."

"Oh, Snowman, you have to remember."

"I know, it's awful. But it will come back to me. I know it will."

It was almost dark now. The late winter sun was sinking weakly behind the southern mountains. The gray smoke was rising wispily from the Scarecrow's house. There was a sense of deeper darkness coming. Real black darkness. The kind of darkness you only get in the winter after a not very bright afternoon, and only in the mountains, when the sky is already hanging low and you can almost feel the light leaving you. It happens this way in the winter when the sun is weak and the clinging light seems almost at times to be coming from the ground. And then when the sun falls it is as if the darkness is coming from the ground.

"You must go back now, Boy, do you hear?"

The Boy turned to go.

"You better come home with me," he said earnestly. "You better come home with me."

The Snowman watched the Boy run down the hill. There could not be much doubt that this Boy must somehow be the one the Old Man had expected. The Snowman remembered the scene so well. The terrible thing was that he had forgotten the key part.

It had happened the winter that the Old Man's son had run off with the girl. It was the boy and the girl who had first made the Snowman. And every year after that they had made him. The Old Man had not been able to believe that they had gone. He had even come that one day to the Peach Tree Hill thinking he would find them with their Snowman. He had come several times. Once he had even talked to the Snowman. The Snowman had never said a word. It just seemed so terrible that no one ever seemed to have any one to talk to.

This one time the Old Man had talked about what a strange old woman fortune-teller had told him about his son. This was what the Snowman could not remember now. It would have to be remembered if he was ever going to tell the Boy who he was.

He knew why he had forgotten it. The old woman's story had been so ridiculous. And the Old Man—the wise Old Man—had believed it so thoroughly. Perhaps because the old woman had been the only person in the world who cared for his fortune. And now the Snowman could not remember.

Chapter 9

There was still the feeding to be done and the wood to carry, but the Boy went up the hill every day to be with the Snowman and to talk of important things. They talked about mountains because there were mountains all around them. They talked about the sky because it was always there. They talked about the earth, how it was round and they were spinning. They decided that if the earth ever stopped spinning they would be dizzy. The Boy told how in summer he would lie flat on his back pressed tight against the curve of the earth and then he was dizzy.

And like all people who talk about important things there were long pauses when they didn't talk about anything, but felt afterwards that they had been talking the whole time constantly. That was how the Boy would sit, hunkering on his heels so the back of him would not get wet, and talk to the Snowman. While the world was spinning with themselves pressed against the curve of it.

But there was one problem. It did come between them. The Boy wanted the Snowman to tell him what he knew, to tell him who he was, to give him the proof. The Snowman could not remember. And he refused to tell him what he could remember. He wanted to put it off. Now was too soon. He and the Boy were having too good a time. All his life, his once-a-year life all these years, he had waited for this—these beautiful golden winter afternoons shared with the Boy, the frost-blue mornings shared with the Boy, and then the farewells when the night pulled the darkness from the ground. . . .

But it did come between them. The Boy did not want to push it—the telling of the story. He did not want the Snowman to think that this was the reason, the real reason, why he came to see him every day. The Snowman didn't want to think that, either.

Yet it came so much between them they didn't talk

about it in any way, not even refer to it. It was too bad. It was one very important thing they didn't talk about.

But they did talk once about the melting. They talked about it one day when the Boy asked the Snowman if it hurt.

"I mean," said the Boy, "does it hurt when it is happening?"

"No, I don't think so," said the Snowman. "I don't think it does because it's as if it were happening to somebody else. You become sort of separated and start to roll off in different directions and you say to yourself (the one it isn't happening to), 'Look you, see what's happening to yourself. You're melting.' Then it happens. The hurt is all in the heart. That never melts. This is the truth."

"I'd be afraid," said the Boy. "It sounds too much like dying."

"That's the way Life is," said the Snowman gloomily.

"That's what the Scarecrow always says. 'That's the way Life is,' " said the Boy, laughing as he gave a very good imitation of the Scarecrow's long face.

The Boy didn't really believe the Snowman would melt, would ever melt. You know how it is in the dead of winter, every winter it happens again, you can't imagine spring or summer. The Snowman was too big, too tall, too distinguished, too white, too wise, too nice to melt. He was there every morning when the Boy came up, always with pipe and hat and cane, looking the same, always the same. Looking just like himself always.

The Snowman interrupted the Boy's thought. "The Thaw will come. And I will melt. But knowing that, I don't miss things. Everything counts with me."

The Boy could not resist, "You don't remember very well."

"But I will," said the Snowman, "I will."

And he did. It was one night after the Boy had gone downhill to the Scarecrow's. It had all come back to him. He remembered the Old Man walking around him talking, telling him what the old woman fortune-teller had said. She had said, "One day, Old Man, a boy with a green chest will come to claim his place."

The Snowman felt relieved. He had remembered. He had been a little afraid that he might not in time. It was late. Sometimes the Thaw came suddenly. You smell it first, warm and sweet. Then the rain came. It was almost as if just then he felt a drop. Then he did hear it coming softly in the mountains—ten thousand million thousand drops falling on the bare branches, onto the snow, each drop making its little dent. He could feel them now, running softly gently down his side to the ground. It was the Thaw, the Big Thaw that ends the winter.

But he must tell the Boy. He must somehow last the night to tell the Boy. For if ever a boy with a green chest were to come then this must be the boy. It simply must be true. There could be no doubt. And the Boy must know. He must be told.

The Snowman wasn't sure which leg moved—but one did. And then the other. He moved slowly and majestically down the hill, stiffly, into the black shadows. Each step he took stiff-legged at a time. The rain came softly on a warm wind. He stopped once to steady himself on a peach tree. He had given up his place on the top of the hill and his view of the world. Here he was lost in the darkness. He went on. Each step less firm. It was harder to see. He lost his cane because he couldn't hold it. And then his eyes fell out. He stopped, threw out his arms to take in all the warm misty world. He was still the Snowman.

It was so dark and slippery. He could feel himself slipping away.

The Scarecrow knew it even as he woke up that morning. There was a warm mist that filled the hollow and the smell of spring was rising from the wet patches of grass—small diamond blotches of palest green around the house and barn—and the cherry tree was standing differently now, as if it were not withdrawn to itself but was reaching. The cherry tree was reaching, and where its branches had been bare the night before because it had lost last year's leaves, now the branches were bare because this year's leaves had not yet come. The snow was melting in the eaves and dripping in the noisy gutter. The snow was sliding off the rocks. The mist was eating the snow from the hills. The ice was splitting. The earth was steaming. The sundial glistened in the ivy and the road reflected the sky.

The Scarecrow let the Boy sleep that morning. Perhaps it wasn't the right thing to do but he couldn't help it. He himself was not going up the Peach Tree Hill today. He couldn't. The Boy would go, of course. And so he let the Boy sleep, hoping that spring would come fast. That it would be there when the Boy awoke.

The Boy knew it the minute he did wake just as the Scarecrow had known it. He could smell it. He could hear it before he looked out his attic window at the green hollow suddenly coming up through the mist.

He rushed on his clothes and without saying "Good morning" or even "Thaw" he was out the door and up the wet, muddy, slippery hill. The Scarecrow didn't even turn to see him go. The Scarecrow could not watch that. Nor even bear to think of it.

"It will be different this year," the Boy said to himself as he ran.

"He will be there. I know it. I know he will. With his pipe and his cane and his hat like always."

Those were the things he saw halfway up the hill. There was no Snowman. Not even a fallen Snowman or a dwindled Snowman. There were only these things. At first the Boy thought that the Snowman must have been washed down here. But then he saw some of the footprints up the hill. He had walked. The Boy knew that he had walked to tell him the story, that he had tried.

He carried the things up the hill. He lay down on the curving top of the spinning world and cried. He cried because he had not been able to keep the Snowman alive. He cried because he had not heard his story. There was no Snowman here now on top of the Peach Tree Hill where the peach trees reached out their bare branches like open hands waiting for their blossoms.

He cried because the man who couldn't talk and couldn't walk could not tell him now.

Chapter 10

Now it is curious how one thing leads to another. On the way down from the Peach Tree Hill that day with the Snowman's hat and cane and pipe and buttons the Boy had picked up a forked branch that was fallen from a peach tree. It caught his eye and so he picked it up and brought it down. It appeared to be some special kind of a branch. Something smooth and brown about it—something wonderful to feel. So he left it in the barn on the way to the house.

It's nice to have a barn to leave things in. Like peach forks. And like special rocks, and snails, and autumn leaves, and feathers, and extra big dead bumble-bees, and bones. All things like that which you don't want to pass up and you need a barn to put them in because the cow doesn't mind or the horse and they don't wonder what—or demand to know what you're going to do with them which is probably nothing.

And so the peach fork lay in the corner of the barn until one afternoon a few days later when the Boy passed through the barn on his way to get the cow for evening milking, saw the peach fork and decided right then and there that he would divine for water on his way to find the cow. You should always *do something* when you are *not doing anything*. Going to find the cow was not really doing anything—

The Boy held the peach tree fork in front of him as he wandered through the meadow. He had heard how it was done. You held the forked end in your two hands and the single end out in front and waited for vibrations. When you walked over water the stick end would, or should, go up and down. He had heard that the power came in part from the wand—ash and hazel and hickory were favored woods—and in part from the diviner himself. The same wand would not work for someone who was not a diviner.

It was one of those first warm evenings of spring when the warmth of the day had lasted on, when the warmth was still there as the chilly evening shadows lengthened. The Boy was on the sheep path that ran along the top of the hill and suddenly he looked across the little cove and saw himself, saw his long-legged shadow on the meadow above the barn. It was the longest-legged shadow he had ever seen. Magnificent. Quite magnificent. As if the world, the universe, the sun, and even the mountains, yes, the mountains, had finally recognized this great, wonderful, magnificent *ME*.

And when he moved a leg the *ME* moved a leg. Just so the Boy danced there his high-stepping dance alone on the hilltop. He regretted that there was no one there to appreciate the size of this shadow he cast over the world. But on the other hand if there had been anyone there to see it, he would not have dared to dance such a ridiculous (to the someone who wasn't there) such a magnificent, high-stepping, kingly (to himself being alone) dance. It was the dance of the Great Diviner.

The Great Diviner realized that he had to give up his shadow. Give up his hilltop shadow to the mountains, to the sunset, to the darkness. Reluctantly, regretfully, he watched himself fade away as he followed the sheep path down off the ridge, and on into the dark woods leading to the Old Man's place. Every once in a while he would pause and stand very still holding the rod in front of him. Nothing happened. Nothing even pretended to happen.

Finally as he sat on the line fence he held out the divining rod, and a thing, yes, a *thing*, did happen. Finally the thing he had been waiting for did happen. But only for an instant. The end of the wand went down. He felt shocks like electric shocks only stronger. Like a fever. The shocks went up his arms, pulsing, pounding at the back of his head, went down his spine ending up tingling in his toes. And then even his ears burned. And he fell off the fence.

When his breath came back the Boy picked up the stick and held it again. The very same thing happened again. Except that he didn't fall off the fence because he was not sitting on it. Now he moved around trying first here and then there. But he always came back to the same place where he had been jounced, to this same saddle of ground, this hump in the earth where the line fence ran between the Scarecrow's property and the Old Man's. No, there could be no doubt about it.

He knelt on the mossed hump that ran along the fence. His knees sunk in the softness and the moss filled his ear. His fingers dug through the copper green to the dark loam where the root veins threaded white. He was kneeling on the humped back of the world. He could hear its insides. He could hear a river rushing dark through long caves where bats flew never touching the walls. Was it their wings beating that he heard? Or the padded walking of blind bears on the slimy rocks? Was this what the peach tree fork had shivered to?

Probably what he heard was the cow approaching. And maybe the roar of that underworld stream was her stomach gurgling. It doesn't matter because it was almost pitch dark now. You shouldn't run a milk cow, particularly if she's on her way to the barn in the evening to be milked, but the Boy did. Down the narrow path she went with tail flying and full udder swinging, big bell clop-clopping from side to side beneath her chin.

Chapter 11

The Boy told the story that night to the Scarecrow, and to the Fox who had just happened to drop by. He had thought that the Scarecrow would be delighted at the idea of finding water but instead he seemed quite terrified of the whole business.

He just muttered. "Don't want water, don't want flies and don't want those fish that ponds have in them. Don't want . . ." He muttered and he moaned and he mumbled but the Fox, on the other hand, who the Boy had thought would be suspicious and scoff, was enthused beyond himself and beside himself. Enraptured—

"I can see it now," he said, striding up and down at a safe distance from the fireplace. "Yes, I can see it clearly, 'The Boy Diviner!' What a ring that has to it! Managed by Mr. Fox, of course. Ah, people will come to us from all over the county. And for a fee, of course, we'll go." Mr. Fox picked up the peach fork. He held it lovingly. His hands trembled.

"Look, oh, look," he said. "It's doing it."

"Oh, no," said the Scarecrow, "*not* in the *house!*"

"It feels like you're on top of a whirlpool," said Mr. Fox.

"Oh, no," said the Scarecrow again, "not under the house!"

"Well, then, must I go it alone, my friends?" said Fox dramatically, putting on his great caped coat.

"I don't think it's right to go digging for anything at this hour," said the Scarecrow.

So pretty soon there went the three of them up the path with their lanterns looking like great fireflies. The Scarecrow insisted that they be tied together like mountaineers or he wouldn't go any farther. A whippoorwill bleated his strange song right out of the ground close by and the Scarecrow jumped and knocked the other two into a scramble and the Fox refused to be tied to the common rope any longer.

Now, every ten feet the Scarecrow would go "Shhh" or whisper "Listen" and they would have to stop. Then the Boy would tug the mountaineer's rope which still bound him and the Scarecrow together and the Scarecrow would jump with fright and start to run like mad until he tripped or wore himself out and had to rest. But they did get there, to the spot, and there they held their lanterns high and while strange shadows lurked and lurched around them the Boy took the rod, held it softly in both hands and—the shock knocked him down. Quite flat. It knocked the wind out of him again, too, but he put up a brave front.

"It didn't electrocute me."

"And maybe knocked some sense into you, too," the Scarecrow said, pulling the poor Boy to his feet.

"That's good enough for me," said Mr. Fox without even looking to see if the Boy was really all right. Just dusted off his paws and set to digging—the dirt flew off his shovel. Right on top of the Boy. Right into the Scarecrow's frightened face. The Fox dug like a fox possessed.

"Listen," said the Scarecrow. "Listen!" And this time there was indeed something to listen to. There was a whirring sound of a great wind—no, not a great wind, a soft slithery withery wind—a flutter and then a shout:

"Look out below, I'm coming down!"

It was the Witch, of course. She had been watching

the sun set. She did this sometimes. She would fly west at twilight sometimes so that night did not come. There were times when she hated night to come. So she flew west, faster and faster. And then there were times when she thought she might even die following the sun to the west, might never get back, but not daring to stop for fear that the night she had left behind would catch up with her. Tonight she had not gone very far west before turning back. Toward the night. She had a funny feeling. It was on her way back that she saw the lanterns and she came down to investigate. She never imagined to find her friend the Scarecrow out gallivanting at such a late hour of such a dark night.

"Pa-shaw!" she said. (She always pronounced the "P" in "Pshaw.") "Divining, will you? Folk superstition! Some people are always so anxious to believe in some magical cause at the bottom of everything. Here, Boy, give me this crazy divining rod." She took the peach fork in her hands and approached the hole challengingly, belligerently. Just as the end of the stick went over the edge it picked up a speed of its own and went right on down in with the Witch following directly behind with black petticoats flying.

"Drop the stick," yelled the Boy, afraid the Witch was going to be suffocated or disappear.

"I can't," said the Witch, muffled from her upside-down position. "I'm being electrocuted!"

"Wonderful, wonderful," said Fox. "That absolutely proves it."

"Oh, the poor dear," said Scarecrow.

"Well, *do* something, somebody!" The Witch went on screaming in muffled, strangled tones, and finally the Boy succeeded in reaching down and getting the stick out of her hands. The stick was stuck to them and her fingers were stuck to it and the fingers would not unstiffen even after the stick was unstuck, but they all pulled her out and set her right way up against the fence and hoped for the best.

"My broom," she said weakly, brushing her skirts. They brought her the broom. "Now please unscrew the broom part (which they did) and be sure to hold the hollow end upright." She could barely move her fingers to open but she held the hollow end to her mouth finally and she took a long draught.

She explained, "Mulberry wine—for crashes."

The Scarecrow was dreadfully concerned. "You shouldn't be doing things like this silly thing at your age, Witch. You could be injured very seriously going into holes like that head first."

It was just then that they saw the long black hat of the Witch which had been left at the bottom of the hole reappear—rise slowly with its crown pointing up until, until . . . They all watched in horror as the hat floated up, floated entirely out of the hole.

And then the water came.

It rose in a great belching gurgling leap out of the ground, it pooled, and then it found its path down the hill onto the Old Man's place. Down went the line fence. Rails were washed away. They could hear the water go, rushing, crashing down the slope of the Old Man's hill.

"Oh, my lord," said the Scarecrow. "This is it."

Even the Fox was overawed. "It might have been better, Boy, to have started with a small one . . ."

"Don't be silly," snapped the Witch. "It's coincidence. The water would have come out, Boy or no Boy." She put on her hat without first looking to see how wet it was. The water ran down her hair. It dropped off her long nose in big drops.

Nobody laughed. You don't laugh at a witch who has just put on a wet dripping hat.

"Let's go home," said the Scarecrow, when she had gone. "And pretend it never happened."

Chapter 12

It was a very serious group which left the house the next morning. The Scarecrow insisted on taking a pail. He was a great believer that where there is a water leak or water seepage you should be prepared to bail.

Mr. Fox was interested only in his camera—one of those large ones with three legs and a bulb you pressed —he had been waiting for something like this for years. He only wished there could be another camera in the county to take a picture of him taking a picture

—his head tucked under the black cloth, his lovely full red bushy tail curling out behind him, the bulb raised imperiously in the air ready to be pressed at the split artistic second.

The Boy had wanted to bring his wand but the Scarecrow wouldn't let him for fear he might find more water and the Fox wanted him to help carry his photography equipment.

If they had stayed up all night imagining they could not have imagined what was really over the hill. Because if you stood at the line fence and looked down over the Old Man's place all you could see for miles and miles was water.

"A lake," said Mr. Fox.

"An ocean," said the Scarecrow, dropping his pail.

"Unbelievable," said the Boy.

The water was not gushing out of the hole now—just a good steady stream. This upper piece of the Old Man's place was a hollow. It was dotted delicately with locust trees and old black willows which grew along a little run called Vinegar Run. This run went on down to the Scarecrow's place. The Scarecrow's hollow was sometimes called Vinegar Hollow. With the water the locusts were more like lily pads now with just their feathery tops showing on top. The hollow was lost. A hollow flooded with water is a lake.

"Fox Hollow Lake, I like that don't you?" said Mr. Fox.

"No jesting, Fox," said the Scarecrow.

"Jesting! Are you blind? Can't you see it now? Hundreds of cottages all around Fox Hollow Lake! Boating, with craft reasonably rented at Commodore Fox's pier!"

It was then that they saw the Witch approaching. She was in good form today, flying precisely, swooping down nicely, then making her pass low over the water. She was so happy. She loved a good natural disaster.

"They did save the town," she said, "but it was touch and go all the way."

"The town? What town?" said the Scarecrow.

"I must say, Boy, you live up to your good name of Flood. Do you know that bridge above Hocky's store?"

"Yup," said the Boy.

"Gone." The Witch let the full import of this sink in. "Do you know the Meetinghouse that used to be at the fork?"

"Used to be?" said the Scarecrow, hoping that the Witch was confused, not really wanting to know any more about these flood conditions.

"Smack up against the front steps of the Lutheran Church. And they're going to sue—both of them."

The Fox had busied himself setting the camera up. "How about one of you, Witch, skimming low over Fox Hollow Lake?"

"I'd just be a blur," said the Witch. "I'd never come out. I'm much too fast. But I do have one idea for a picture. Look there!" And there tied at the edge of the water was a small boat.

"Watch," said the Witch.

She whisked over to it, attached her broom at the propeller place and pretty soon she was tearing around and round the lake in her version of an outboard (outbroom) motorboat.

Tuesday it was when the lake appeared. So, of course, it was Wednesday when everybody appeared. People all over the county woke up and said to each other that morning, "This is the day. Let's go see that brand-new lake."

Everybody came. By wagon and by horse and by foot. Families. Lovers. People from town. The other people. The Old Man came and rode around the lake on his horse without saying a word to anyone, sitting very straight as always and taking care to keep clear of the children playing at the edge.

(The Old Man had lived much of his life on horse and there had been several and he had outlived them all. Each one dying had meant a little less, but he knew the handling of a horse and he could make one he knew walk in a flower bed without hurting the flowers just as now he could make this one walk high so as not to step on the children playing at the edge. It was as if he walked among them himself with four legs.)

Nobody had been allowed on the property where the lake appeared in years. All these people were trespassing now but the Old Man had enough sense not to make a case of it. This was too special a day. How often does a lake appear? Particularly in limestone country where there are no lakes.

For most people this was the only lake they had ever seen. The men speculated on how many gallons it was, on how deep it was, how cold, how many acres it covered. The women didn't say things like that. They said things like how strange it made you feel to have all this water come up like this and how peaceful it made you feel. There was a pair of lovers and the boy made the girl very upset by asking how many gallons she thought it was and how deep and how cold it was. She said, "Oh, Johnny, just look at it, will you, just look at how it's blue with the sky—and us, you can see us in it," and she hugged him tight while he wished he was better at arithmetic and remembered how you go from gallons to square feet.

The Witch, who had always said that she didn't like children, even took several of the little people as she called them into her boat and they loved it. They sat in front, very still. They knew the Witch was supposed to not like little children and so they were most careful. With hands in laps. Not to rock the boat. Away they zoomed—in and out of the floating treetops looking like lily pads, zoom, zoom.

The Scarecrow had been up at the lake earlier. But he had gone home with a baby deer, two baby rabbits, and a baby snake. All of them had been run out of their homes by the lake. It was so depressing. Nobody cared. He gave the baby deer a bottle that he used for orphan lambs. He let the baby rabbits suck milk off his finger.

The snake was more of a problem. Finally he gave it a saucer of cream with granddaddy flies in it. He swatted the flies viciously with an old slipper. He felt so alone. And in the meantime the Witch was making a fool of herself in the boat and the Boy was acting as if he were a fish.

This was exactly what was going on. The Boy had discovered skin diving. It was the Witch who had made it possible. She had given him her glasses (the ones without any glass) and explained to him that with these he would have no problems at all under water. And it was the way it had worked out. He didn't even have to breathe, it seemed. Sometimes he did come up, but that was mainly to see where he was in relation to the rest of the world.

The rest of the time he stayed under water. It was wonderful. He would follow a tree trunk down into the dark depths where only rays of light came in and there was no sound. And the briars covered the bottom in a waving sea of green.

It was while he was under water that the Witch

took on a new rider. The little children were returned to shore—all with very stiff backs from that military posture and with very hoarse throats. Not many people saw it the way it happened but everybody will tell you now how they remember seeing the Old Man walk his horse slowly along the edge of the lake. You couldn't hear what the Witch said but a number of people said they saw him tip his hat and nod his head in a courtly way. Then he got in the boat.

The Old Man sat up very straight in the boat facing the Witch—not out of respect like the straight-backed little children but because he always did. The Witch also sat up very straight with a smile on her face and she talked a blue streak. The boat was entirely enveloped in a blue haze and the Witch drove the boat so fast it churned up whitecaps and the two of them out there in the middle of the lake looked as if they were floating in a summer's sky.

The faster she talked the faster the Witch drove the boat. In fact, the Old Man took off his hat and kept it in his lap.

Way out in the middle of the lake the Witch stopped the boat and let it drift. She leaned over and pointed down. The Old Man looked over. It was hard to see. But there were the green briars at the bottom and there moving through the green milky light was a slim figure. It was the naked figure of the Boy moving slimly in slow motion above the waving green briars.

"It's a green boy," she said.

Together they watched him move through the water, saw him caught for an instant in a shaft of sunlight, and then lost out of sight in the green swirl.

The Old Man sat up very straight. He put on his fine hat and he wasn't smiling. He looked grim when the Witch brought him back to the water's edge. He got out with only a bare thank-you (the Witch looked crestfallen). He was preoccupied. He mounted his horse. The Witch watched him.

Out in the middle of the lake the Boy surfaced for a look around. He saw them and waved. The Old Man hesitated a moment and waved back.

He turned to the Witch with a surprised smile. "It's the Boy, isn't it? He was the one down there in the green water."

"Who else?" said the Witch.

"I don't know," said the Old Man. "I don't know."

He rode off along the water's edge. This Boy meant something to him. It had been true from the first day they had met at the calf's birth. They had met but a few times since then, but always they had acknowledged each other. It had been a long time since the Old Man had acknowledged anyone. That meant for the eyes to meet. That meant to wonder suddenly that there was another person in the world.

Chapter 13

The Boy was lying in the shade at the edge of the pasture on the hill looking down on the fields. It was summer now. The heat waves came up dizzy from the wet ground. The air was warm and sweet but not sleepy. There were no animals in sight on the fields below. The Boy sensed the cows above him in the shade like himself. He could see the sheep across the hill panting white on the bare ground beneath the maples where the grass never grew. The bare roots ran like snakes over the dusty ground. The summer had taken over. Only the bees moved.

It had been a long climb up the hill and now as he lay still the drops ran down his forehead, down his nose, and he caught them salty one by one and ate them. And he waited. He watched the dancing heat waves on the pasture and he felt coiled to spring, to rush down the hill when the Caravan appeared. The horses would dance high with silver feet and the gold would spill in heavy orange slippery dollars. He would dip his arms in them to the elbow. Barrels of perfume would burst. Velvet pillows would fall from over-turned wagons and he would shout in strange languages, "*Abo bis yatsin*" and things like that.

"Hello," a voice suddenly interrupted him. It was a little boy standing very small with one hand resting on a large dog's back. "I'm from over the mountain. Are you looking for another lake?"

"No."

"I never came over the mountain before by myself."

"I guess it's a long way."

"It's the first time I've done it." The little boy pointed down the valley. "You live here?"

"Yes, I live here with the Scarecrow."

The little boy shook his head. "I don't know him at all. I think Alexandra knows him. Alexandra knows a lot of people I don't know. My name is Jamie and this is Luke. He belongs to my sister, but he's too dirty for her." He looked down the valley where the small hills rolled against each other and the rail fences snaked silver-gray across the pasture. "It's pretty nice on this side of the mountain, but I have to go back."

"I'll go with you." They walked together up the path through the woods. Jamie was getting tired. Every once in a while he would stop and fold his arms across his chest and sigh very seriously in answer to a question asked a long time ago. He was getting his breath. Finally he agreed to be carried piggyback and they went on like that.

"Poor Luke," he said. "There's nobody to carry poor Luke. But I'll do it someday, I'll carry Luke all around like this. You'd like it up here, Luke. It's where the branches are."

"Luke would be hot to carry," said the Boy.

"He wouldn't know how probably to hang on like I do. Luke pants." Jamie panted—oh-ah-oh—and nearly fell off.

"Be careful," said the Boy, too sharply.

Jamie was suddenly very still and not even wiggly. He put his head soft against the Boy's shoulder and it joggled lifelessly.

The Boy caught Jamie tighter with his arms. He said nothing. It was too bad. It always seemed to happen with children that you found yourself acting grown up, or felt you should.

The path took them on a slanting way up the mountain until almost at the top the pines began. A grove of great white pines. There was no brush now or small trees, only the great red trunks of the pines rising branchless to way, way up where the branches began and reached across to each other and made a ceiling. It was dark and shadowless here and no other smell but pine.

"This is Alexandra's room," Jamie said, pointing to a great corridor running along the top of the mountain. The ground was only pine needles. Here and there were large pine cones fallen from their pinnacles where the wind roared through the branches like the ocean.

"Is Alexandra your sister?"

Jamie nodded. "Nobody will ever change that. Alexandra is my sister. She comes here." Jamie pointed to a flower bed. Row on row of flowers grown without sunlight. All white on long pale stems with great white petals. Each row was staked and lettered and numbered neat.

"They don't smell," Jamie said. "They don't even smell for Alexandra."

When they started down the mountain Jamie said, "Maybe you better not come home with me."

"Why not?"

"Alexandra doesn't like strange people. She shoos them away."

"How about your mother?"

"I don't have a mother. I have a father and he makes fireworks."

"You mean all the time? That's what he does?"

"That's what he does." The Boy could feel Jamie nodding. "All the time."

"And shoots them off, too?"

"Other places. He goes away and shoots them off. He has—my father has a barn—like this—it's so big and full of fireworks that if one went off maybe the whole world would be like a fireworks. I don't go in there."

"That would be something."

"He has some fireworks that he's *never* going to shoot off, he says. They're too beautiful."

"How does he know if he's never seen them?"

"He knows."

They could see the small farm now at the bottom of the mountain and white chickens about the house. The garden plot stood out square and rich apart from the house with the corn on one end and the rows of cabbage and maybe string beans in the middle or peas. Somebody in a blue dress was working in the garden.

"That's Alexandra. . . . I would never go in that barn."

They were coming down the mountain sharply now and Luke was way ahead. When he barked, Alexandra turned to see them and came running toward them.

"I don't think you want to meet Alexandra," said Jamie.

But it was too late to do anything before Alexandra

was upon them. She had black hair tight with a white part down the middle. Dark eyebrows. Big dark brown eyes. "Where have you been, Jamie?"

"Nowheres."

"Well, get down anyway and come along."

The Boy watched them go. He knew to himself that Alexandra was going to turn around. If she did he was going to come to this side of the mountain again, and if she didn't he wouldn't.

She didn't.

Chapter 14

It was a few days later that he first went back. He followed the same path up the mountain, through the pine woods, past the white flowers. He could imagine Alexandra here. He knelt now to see the flowers closer and cupped his hands about the blooms. Is this what she did here? If this were his room he would carve things on the trees. He would build castles out of pine cones.

That first day he didn't go all the way down to the farm. He watched it from the mountain. He watched Alexandra go to the garden. He watched the father go to the barn. He watched Jamie swing on the pear tree by the house.

The next time Luke came to meet him and Jamie took him around. There were two milk cows and quite a few sheep. The two Dorset bucks had a small pasture of their own. Sometimes they butted heads.

It was something Jamie never got tired of. They would sit on the fence.

"Oh, they're going to do it," Jamie would say.

The two rams would back away from each other, pawing the ground as they went, shaking their heads gently from side to side, balancing their wonderful regal brown-ivory ridged horns that curved away and up from the heads.

They pawed. Then suddenly ran blindly at each other.

"Thunk," the heads met. The backs arched and sometimes both front feet came entirely off the ground.

"Thunk," echoed Jamie happily.

Then the bucks would roll their heads drunkenly, back up again, not quite so far, and come together again not quite so fast.

"Thunk," the heads met.

"Thunk," said Jamie. "That was a good one."

The bucks would stagger off in different directions —calmed, soothed.

"It makes my head hurt," said Jamie rubbing the top

of his head. And he jumped off the fence and took up his position opposite Luke. He pawed the ground, "Luke, here I come," and he hurled himself at the dog, who knocked him down. "Thunk, thunk, thunk."

As they sat there they saw Alexandra go down past the large meadow. She was carrying a small white sack. She was walking with head down swinging the sack. Her black hair glistened.

"Alexandra, she's in a dudgeon," said Jamie.

"How come?"

"It's her deer. They're some deer down there past the meadow. She's going down there now to give them salt."

"So?"

"Last year we had extra hay and Alexandra gave it to the deer, but we don't have any this year and Father told her she couldn't."

"Pretty deer, are they?"

"They're all right. They don't bump heads. Alexandra says they do. But I never saw them."

"Let's go see them."

"Alexandra won't like it. She said not even to tell you about them. She said you'd want to shoot them."

"I don't want to shoot any deer. I'm peaceful."

"That's what I told her. She said, all boys are the same anyway."

The Boy slid down from the fence. "I'm going down there."

"Don't you tell her I told you."

"I won't."

He followed her path past the big meadow where the hay was up nicely now—golden-brown orchard grass and down below the thick undergrowth of red clover. The breeze stroked the meadow with a big hand. Beyond the meadow the cove widened out to a nice pasture. He could see Alexandra ahead. She went all the way across the pasture to a big flat rock at the edge of the woods. She poured out the salt and spread it out. She whistled a good high trill that carried into the woods. The birds laughed and changed places with one another in the trees. The deer came out of the woods in dignified haste, long-legged, picking their way across the rocky pasture to the salt rock. They took long serious licks, raising their heads to savor it. They paid no attention to Alexandra when she came up to stroke them except for the little ones who danced high away. A buck came out of the woods now. And Alexandra moved away. Bucks can be mean. He moved in, shouldering the others aside for his greedy licks.

The Boy stood where he was by a tree not moving. Leaning hard against it so that he might become part of it. He never moved even when Alexandra saw him and walked back toward him.

"What are you doing here?"

"I was just watching."

She didn't seem to hear. They stood there together. She was sort of like a deer. He had never seen her like this. She had been so matter of fact. It was almost as if she had come away a deer and did not want to rejoin her people—like him.

He almost said, "He's some buck," but he caught himself because she would think that he wanted to shoot it. "He might have butted you."

"He might."

"He's used to running things."

"I like the does best. They're so quiet and dainty." She smoothed her hair. She had come back.

They walked together back to the house. The minutes were going by so fast that he could feel them going out at the end of his finger tips.

"The meadow looks good, doesn't it? You'll have to mow it soon." He stopped and leaned against the fence, hoping she would stop and give him time to think.

She did. "But we don't have as much hay as last year. We're keeping more sheep this year and I don't know what the deer are going to do. We've always had extra hay to give them. And this year we don't."

"Maybe you could find some hay someplace, maybe an old field you could fence in."

She shook her head.

He wished that he could snap his fingers and deliver her a haystack. His mind raced across the country.

Someplace there was some hay he would find for her. And then it came to him. It was a small field on the mountain surrounded by vines too thick for anything to get in. "I know where there's some hay. I know right where. Up on the mountain."

"Do you?"

"It's not very far. Come on. I'll show you." He took her by the hand.

"No," she said. "You're teasing."

He dropped her hand.

"I'll come," she said, "you lead."

He raced ahead. He knew right where to go, up the path toward the pine trees and then to the right across a bare shaley place. It was slippery here and he had to stop for Alexandra to catch up. And then they came to the vines—a wall of vines against the trees, entangled like stone snakes. The leaves were big and dark with diseased brown spots. Strange bugs dropped like pebbles.

And then they came to it. A small field of red clover like a garden. An old snake fence stood entwined in vines about the meadow. Alexandra held out her hands as if she would pick up the whole field and hold it to herself. "And all this time it was here by itself."

"It's all clover," he said. He had been so afraid that it wouldn't be here, that it would be grown up, that it would have been discovered, that it would have vanished. And he had found it all for her. "We'll cut a path. We'll mow it, we'll stack it there and we'll fence it. Then this winter the deer can stay here and you can let them go to the stack. It wastes hay, but it's all right."

"But how will we make hay up here? I know my father won't let his mower up."

"I'll do it. I'll get a mower up here and we'll mow it."

He could see it now—this haystack standing alone in the secret field within the vine walls that he had found.

Chapter 15

The Scarecrow was not happy about the idea. "It's the Old Man's property."

"He'll never know," said the Boy. "He hasn't been up there in years."

"Oh, I don't know. What do you think, Mr. Fox?" asked the Scarecrow. "It seems to me ill advised."

"We could have a picnic," said the Boy. "And the deer, think of the deer."

Mr. Fox was lying on the lawn with one leg cocked over a raised knee and his hat pulled down over his face. He often took this position after a big dinner when he didn't want anybody to know that he was dozing.

It was just then that Alexandra appeared around the corner of the house. She stood there shyly not expecting to find such a group. The Scarecrow was most flustered and insisted on her taking the rocker. "This is a pleasure," he kept saying.

"We are delighted," said the Fox.

It was amazing how possessed Alexandra was. She just rocked back and forth and complimented the Scarecrow on his property and in particular the wisteria.

"I don't think I've seen you since you were a little girl," said the Scarecrow. "I just never go over the mountain. And I should."

"I came," she said, "because of the field. That field belongs to the Old Man. And I don't think . . ." she couldn't finish. "I was so happy . . . and now I'm so unhappy."

"There now . . . there now," said the Scarecrow. He pulled out a big red handkerchief and gave it to Alexandra.

"But, of course, the property belongs to the Old Man," the Boy said. He didn't even know what he was going to say next. "And the Scarecrow has had it leased for years."

"There is no problem, my dear," said the Fox expansively. "This is an old arrangement that goes back many, many years—before you or I were born. It's not spoken of, not known of. Tax purposes," he added mysteriously.

"Uh," said the Scarecrow. "Hardly known of at all, but, uh, it's as Mr. Fox said." He couldn't do anything else but continue the lie, for Alexandra had wiped away her tears and was looking at him with big admiring brown eyes.

"I want to kiss you," and she threw her arms around him and hugged him tight.

"Yes," said the Scarecrow. "Of course. I'm obliged." It was going to take a long time to get his straw back in place after this hug.

"It's so wonderful," Alexandra said, rocking back. She sighed. "That wisteria." She rocked once, twice. "Well," she said. "I should not keep you."

She turned once at the garden gate. "You better come home with me." In the half-light her white dress billowing filled the eye like the sun.

"Good night, good night," they waved.

"A whirlwind," said the Scarecrow collapsing in his rocker. "What have we done?"

Almost every day the Boy looked at the meadow. It was all red clover and it had to be mowed at exactly the right time. It had to be just when maybe a third of the bloom was gone. It would never dry if you cut it too green. There would be no tenderness if you cut it too late.

The morning came. They met early at the meadow —the Boy, Scarecrow, and Fox from their side of the mountain and Alexandra, Jamie, and Luke from their side. Rain could not fall on this hay. It must be cut first thing—as soon as the dew had gone—then it would dry and be ready to put up that afternoon. The secret was to get it down early so that it could be put up the same day.

The weather was unknown. The morning mist was still about them now. It weighted down the spider webs hanging silkily between the fence rails around the meadow. The hay was bent with dew. The water stood in drops on the oily mower. The air smelled of wet clover and wet pines and wet rails. The dew dropped noisily from leaf to leaf in the vines.

Even as they stood there the world grew larger about them. The wall of vines above the meadow became warm with light. Luke shook showers of diamonds from his back. It could hardly be that this was the beginning of one day. It could hardly be that the mist would not rise to reveal a new world—with a mountain taller than the one the sun had set behind the night before, with a valley stretching further than remembered.

The mist went. The light came. The ghosts disappeared from behind the tree trunks. Gravestones turned into rocks. Long arms turned into branches and herds of humped things were lost in briar patches.

It was like standing on the tip of a candle.

The mist was gone and the world was blue.

"Let's make hay," cried the Boy. Into the meadow they went. The Boy rode the mower. He cut the first swath with the end of the mower just slipping past the fence posts. Then the next swath he cut back in the opposite direction and all the other swaths round and round like that so that he always had the mower in the hay. Alexandra walked behind clearing a little path with her fork so that the mower would not get clogged in the old swath.

The mower bar shuttled back and forth clicking, snipping. The short red-blossomed clover grass fell in waves over the mower. The swaths lay in neat long red-dusted green blankets. It was hot now in the tiny meadow. The Boy took off his shirt. His tight chest glistened brown. Alexandra walked quickly, head down behind the mower, clearing the path, her arms bedecked with red seed. Her white kerchief had fallen about her neck.

The Scarecrow and the Fox scythed down the hay in the v's of the rail fence where the mower could not reach. Sweep—the blades silvered through the grass. Every once in a while they stopped to stone the blade. The old blades, thinned and shortened by years of stoning, arched in silver crescents. Then sweep—they would swing through. Queen Anne's lace grew in the corners and smelled bitter, cut. Jamie came after and raked the hay from the corners.

It was really hot now. The heat seemed to come even from the ground. The sweetness of the hay came up rich with the full store of a year—ten feet of snow, a hundred rains, the harvest of other years grown and rotted here in this secret meadow.

When it was done they stopped and looked around. They walked through the hay and kicked it. The grasshoppers popped through the air.

In the shade they prepared the picnic—opening the baskets, unwrapping and sniffing. The people from one side of the mountain peered curiously into the baskets from the other side of the mountain. Everybody had three hands.

It was then that the Witch appeared, swooping in from the west, hovering for a moment above the red-topped carpet and then landing softly. She kicked the hay with a peaked shoe. "Haven't we done well," she said. "Where's the food?"

They lay in the shade and ate their lunch. They sent Jamie back and back to the spring for water. Alexandra took another helping of the Scarecrow's apple butter and said it was delicious. The Scarecrow took another helping of Alexandra's pickles made by herself and described them as out of this world. The Fox lay on his back with one knee up to look alive. Jamie stood on his head and everyone worried about his stomach going upside down. The Witch told the story about old lady Harris who had liked green cabbage. She ate a lot for lunch one day and afterwards lay in the sun and went to sleep. She blew up. Alexandra sat against a tree with her yellow dress spread like a fan. And they sat about her.

"We must do this every year," said the Scarecrow. "It's the kind of day you never forget."

The Boy wandered off to kick the hay. It was dry on top but underneath it was still damp and green. "All right, everybody up. We've got to turn the hay." They each got a fork and went down the swaths flipping the hay over. Jamie and the Witch sat on the fence and shouted at anyone who was maybe too quick and missed some.

Then came the setting of the pole. The Boy had cut a good locust pole days ago and now there was only the hole to dig, the pole to be set in. And when it was done they stopped and admired the pole standing up so high and clear in the middle of the meadow. The Scarecrow used his fork handle as a plumb and pronounced that it stood straight. Maybe it could go a little to the right. The Boy hammered the left brace a little tighter. That was good.

Now the hay had to be raked by hand. The path up the mountain was too narrow for the hay rake. Then it had to be shocked. Piled in small stacks. The

Scarecrow tended to make wide-based shocks and not so high. The Witch made a good real big firm shock. When she finished one she gave it a no-nonsense tap on the top with her fork as a test. Alexandra's were small and a little toppy. When she wasn't looking the Scarecrow might take two of hers and make them into one good one. Finally it was done. The shocks stood in haphazard rows on the bare stubble waiting.

They were ready to build the stack, but who was to be the builder? The builder is the one who stands at the pole tramping down the hay as it is piled on. That is the easy part. But as the stack goes up, the builder is the one who shapes it, who says that this should go there and that should go here. It was agreed that the Fox and the Boy would have to pitch. The Scarecrow said that he could not possibly take the responsibility of building. The Witch said that she was going to ride the horse with Jamie and bring in the shocks. Alexandra said she never had built a stack, but she would.

The Witch and Jamie rode the horse to a shock. The Scarecrow took the drag chain and hooked it around the bottom of the shock. It was dragged to the stack. Then they went back for another. The Fox and the Boy pitched the hay about the stack.

It was slow at first. Most of a haystack is in the base. Gradually it started up until it was over their heads and Alexandra looked down at them and called them slowpokes. The butt of a stack is easy. It's the bringing it in from there to the top that's hard. It has to be sloped in just right—not so steep it might blow over, not so flat it will hold water and rot. The Boy had the long finishing fork now, twice as long as the regular fork. He only pitched a little at a time. Alexandra showed him where she wanted it. Maybe there was a place here that was coming in too sharp, but nobody said anything. Only one person can build a stack. And Alexandra didn't ask them either. She just caught the hay from the Boy's fork on her own and slid it into place.

Finally the last shock came in and the others sat down on the stubbled field to watch. There was not much room for Alexandra to stand now. The stack had not had time to settle and it wobbled. Each forkful had to be placed just right now. Sometimes Alexandra would move one just a touch, getting it right so that the slope was smooth.

"How much is left?" she asked.

"About five or six good forks."

"I couldn't use more."

"You better not. There isn't any more."

"No, it's all right. But here I need some."

"We have to save some for the collar."

The Boy took the little hay that was left and rolled it into a heavy rope and knotted it like a collar. This went on the very top to keep the water from going down around the pole and rotting the hay. He put the collar on the end of his fork and handed it up. With one hand hanging on to the pole Alexandra reached out and pulled it off. Then standing on her tiptoes, her brown legs gleaming, she put it over the top of the pole.

It was finished.

The Boy stepped back. His arms ached and his neck was cricked forever from looking up. He stepped a good ways back and for the first time saw the stack standing in its solitary splendor in the center of the field, green and red-dotted. It quivered. Alexandra stood with one hand about the pole looking down at them.

"Is it all right?" she shouted down. "How does it look? I bet it's crooked."

"No," said the Scarecrow, "it's perfect."

"You're perfect," said the Fox. "You'll have to stay up there."

"Alexandra can't get down. Alexandra can't got down," chanted Jamie.

"I don't want to come down. I want to stay up here forever. I can see so far from here." The meadow itself was in shadow now. Only Alexandra was in the sun. Her black hair was like a crow's wing. Her yellow dress hung still. She hugged the pole, her cheek against it. The Boy wondered what Alexandra could see from there that made her so different. She had gone so far beyond them. She seemed to grow bare-legged out of the haystack into the sun.

"Alexandra can't get down. Alexandra can't get down," chanted Jamie.

"Here I come." She flung her fork far away from them. It stuck in the ground and the handle quivered back and forth.

The Boy propped the long pitching fork against the side of the haystack for her to slide down. He held it tight. Down she came against him. Still warm from her pinnacle. Girls were soft.

And then she was Alexandra again. She danced around the haystack. She and the Scarecrow held hands and danced around the haystack. Jamie followed. Luke barked.

Chapter 16

The next day the Boy went up to fence the haystack.
It had settled some, grown squatter overnight. Already
it had found its place. It wasn't something they had
built. It was something that had always been there—
rising curved and shaggy from the slanting meadow.
No matter what side he looked at it from it was right.
He burrowed his arm deep inside. If hay is put up too
green it will get hot. Sometimes in a barn it might
catch on fire. A haystack will only mold. It was good.
It was warm. With the tips of his fingers he could feel

the blossoms deep inside and he wished that he could follow them to the very center of the warmth.

It was when he was carrying rails to the stack that he saw the Old Man riding up the mountain. The Old Man was still far below with his back to him. He could not yet have seen the stack but he would when he got to the top.

The Boy ran to meet him. Somehow the Old Man must not see the stack.

Just before they met the Boy stopped running and began to saunter.

"Oh, hello," said the Old Man surprised. "We meet again. You seem to like my property."

"Oh, I was just passing through." He got more breath back. "It's a nice day, isn't it?"

"Yes, it is." The Old Man looked down at him. "It's a long way from Ohio, isn't it?"

"Yessir."

"I understand you lost your family in the Ohio flood. Is that right?"

The Boy fingered the ring around his neck. He would show it to him.

But he didn't have a chance. The Old Man went on. "Yes, that was a very great flood. Of course, you don't remember it at all. Well, come along. Let's look at the top of the mountain together."

Up they went together along the narrow path side by side. The Old Man's boots were as old as he was with scars crisscrossed black with years of polish. "I used to come here all the time," he said. "I even made hay up here. Would you believe it? And now I haven't been up here in years."

The Boy's heart was dry in his mouth. In a few more steps they would be at the top. "Look," he said, "down there—there's a man with a gun."

"Where?" The Old Man turned slowly. "Where? I can't see. Your eyes are better than mine, Boy."

"Down there—in the birches." The Boy ran down the path as fast as he could. He could hear the Old Man coming behind him. The hooves were sharp clicks on the rocks.

The Boy ran off the path and into the thick grove of white birches. "You better leave the horse here, sir."

"All right."

"I saw him go through here."

The Old Man dismounted slowly. "All right. Don't rush me, Boy. We'll get him."

They picked their way carefully through the trees. The Old Man seemed much older now without his horse. He bowed slowly beneath the white arched branches as he made his way. "I hope you know what you're doing, Boy."

The Boy circled around behind the Old Man. Now was his chance. He was off and running back to the path. Untied the horse. Pulled himself into the saddle.

His feet did not reach the stirrups and he hung on with his knees.

"Boy! Boy!" He could hear the Old Man. He was dimly aware of the Old Man moving slowly back through the white trees with one hand outstretched. "Where are you going?"

The words echoed. "Where are you going? Where are you going?" The wind bit at the Boy's eyes and watered them.

"I'm going. I'm going," he cried back as he rattled down the mountain scattering rocks below him. The rocks bounced and skipped through the brush. A covey of quail burst into the air.

The Boy looked back once to where the Old Man stood alone on the path. His hat was gone. He stood bareheaded, white like the birches.

The Boy pressed the horse faster. "Where are you going? Where are you going?" the wind whispered past his ear.

It had been a long day. He had left the Old Man's horse at the county line store and told them the Old Man would be by to pick it up. And then he had walked. He had stopped once for food. He didn't have much money and he knew he had to be practical so he bought two licorice sticks and a jar of peanut butter. And for a while he felt like a king.

But now with his back against a tree he just felt alone. It had only been yesterday that they made the haystack. It was only this morning that he had stolen the Old Man's horse. He had looked back once on the town where it lay on the valley floor like white matchboxes. When night came he had reached the mountain beyond, and it was much much colder up here than you'd guess, and he did not know where he was going, except that he must walk the night to get there.

He didn't even hear the Witch arrive. "Ah," she said, "I've found you. I knew I would."

"He didn't find the haystack, did he, Witch?"

"No," she shook her head, "he didn't, but I don't know how smart it was to leave him up there on the mountain. He came down awful mad."

"I didn't know what to do."

"The important thing is what to do now."

"I can't go back."

"Of course you can," said the Witch heartily. "I tell you what. I don't ordinarily do it, but I'll give you a ride back on the broom. Only you must promise never to mention it to anyone."

"It won't work, Witch. You know it won't."

"He is pretty mad," she admitted. "But cheer up." She took another tack. "Think of the places you can go—California, or anywhere."

"I don't want to go anywheres."

The Witch was silent. She understood in a way. She liked to be going anywheres, to not know where you're going when you set out.

"You could go to California and divine for gold."

"I suppose."

"You could go to the Pacific and be a sailor. Or an admiral."

The Boy looked into the end of the world between his knees.

"You could be a soldier. You could be a general. You could go to Spain and kill bulls." The Witch made a sweep with her cape and neatly stuck the bull between the shoulders as he passed by.

She wrapped the cloak around herself again. "You could be," she said, "almost anyone."

"You'll take care of them, won't you?" said the Boy. "Witch, you take care of the Scarecrow and the Fox."

"I'll keep them in line."

"They need you to watch things up, Witch."

"And how about you, Boy, think about it again?"

"No, Witch, no. I just realized something and it's no changing or even thinking about. I don't belong here. You can't stay where you don't belong. I'm going to go somewheres and be somebody."

The Witch nodded sadly. "But before you go, I want to give you a going-away present. Something to eat? You want something to eat? All boys like to eat.

Or your fortune? I can tell fortunes. I love to tell fortunes."

"No, thank you."

"How about—I could be a bird for you, bring you berries, I could be a monkey. . . ."

"A bear? Could you be a bear?"

"I could be a bear."

"A polar bear. Could you be a polar bear?"

"A white polar bear. I could be that. Now you wait. You go over there by that tree and you wait. Just close your eyes and wait. Just stay and wait until you know I've had a chance."

The Boy did, did wait. He went over to the tree and leaned against it and he waited. With the ridges of the bark hard on his cheek. He closed his eyes and his head went spinning with the memories of the Fox and of the Scarecrow and Alexandra—and of the Old Man, too —he could see them all so clearly. His head went spinning and spinning and then it seemed to come to a perfectly still stop and he knew that the Witch had had time. There was this white polar bear coming slowly toward him on big padding paws with a pink muzzle and white teeth and a long pink tongue. The Boy kneeled to meet the bear and hugged her around the neck. The bear cuffed him. They wrestled. The enormous bear and the Boy. He put his whole hand in the warm mouth and felt the teeth against his wrist and finally went to sleep curled up there against the white fur—the wonderful long white fleece that rose and fell slowly like the tide around him. He was all entirely surrounded by wonderfully soft animal fur that smelled warm and sweet and he went fast asleep.

The Old Man eased his horse up the mountain path toward the Devil's Backbone and then over the ridge and on down into the forest on the other side. He was sure that this was the way the Boy had come. He would find him. It was cold in the late night. The wild rhododendron drooped black along the side of the road and the lichen was dusted with hoarfrost. The tree owls mourned. The darkness shook the pine boughs. The stars pricked out clean and bright in the late night's sweet chill air. A wildcat screamed for all the living.

The Old Man held his rifle firmly. When you're a young man you can hold a rifle loosely and you have a grip but when you're an old man and your hands are not good any more you will drop it.

The Boy was still fast asleep when the first white rays of morning light silvered the sky. The wind was still singing and sighing in the pine needles and the white bear sighed with almost a sob as she stood up on her great haunches. The big head hung loosely from the huge white shoulders. The pink muzzle rubbed the boy's cheek and the big tongue tickled his ear. The Boy sneezed but did not wake. The white bear moved her paws away from the sleeping Boy very delicately and once she was quite free she lumbered away. But not far. She was waiting. She was waiting for something. She went back to the Boy and stood over him.

The Boy was dreaming out loud again. "Could you be a polar bear?"

The bear put her great head down. "I could be a polar bear," she said softly. She stood still with all four feet over the Boy so that he was completely hidden. Then she lifted her head toward the sky and sniffed the breeze and waited for the sound of the horse to come closer.

As the Old Man came around the turn in the road he *saw*. The rifle came easily from its scabbard and the metal was cold and smelled of oil against his cheek. The trigger was alive.

There were no white bears in this world. He watched it go—lumbering off on padded paws into the woods.

It happened to be Saturday afternoon when the town was full. Children were playing around the statue in front of the Courthouse and the men were sitting on the Courthouse steps and the ladies were scattering especially in and out of Mr. Nagle's store. It was a perfectly ordinary Saturday until the MacDonalds' wagon came swooping into town. MacDonald Senior pulled on his reins to stop at the Courthouse and said "Go" when he meant "Whoa" and the horses reared up and sideways. The wagon almost keeled over. The ladies muttered to each other that he was drunk again and that woman. . . .

Everybody crowded around to hear the news.

The MacDonald children told the children around the statue. The women of the family walked tight-lipped down to Mr. Nagle's store where they passed out the news embellished like a pie at a church supper.

But all the MacDonald clan told pretty much the same story. They had passed the Old Man coming down the mountain with the Boy. The Boy was on the horse with him. Both of them covered with dust. The Old Man did not look their way even but kept that old black hat pulled down over his face. The big horse was tired with a limping foot.

One of the MacDonald boys said that he was sure the Boy was dead. "I looked right at him, too. And you know how a dead lamb lies with a twisted head. That's the way he was, I swear."

Then someone shouted, "Here they come."

And there they came. Down the dusty mountain from the west. The men sitting on the Courthouse steps leaned forward some. The children climbing up the statue of Columbus clung where they were. The ladies in Nagle's store stood still in the doorway.

Pretty soon you could see the Boy very quiet maybe dead very small and thin mounted up in front of the Old Man who had furled his long cape around them so it covered them both. They had come from the mountain where it was cold down into the warm valley and they had not noticed. Nor did they seem to notice anything.

"He's going to take him to jail," said the MacDonald boy. People made way for the Old Man to turn in there, but he didn't. He kept on going past the Courthouse and the store and then out of town in the direction of his farm.

"He's going to bury him at his farm," said the Mac-Donald boy, who was going to somehow make this a real Saturday afternoon.

"He isn't dead, boy," said his father. "They're just going home."

About the Author

Several of the characters in *You Better Come Home with Me* came to life in stories that John Lawson told to his children when they were young. The background of this book grew from the five years Mr. Lawson and his family lived on a farm in the mountains of Virginia.

A native of New York City, John Lawson was graduated from Exeter and Harvard College. During World War II, he served with the Army in France and Germany. Mr. Lawson is now in the brokerage business, and lives in Westchester, New York, with his wife and two daughters.

About the Illustrator

Arnold Spilka is well known for his illustrations of children's books, and his delightful drawings perfectly match the mood of each text he illustrates.

Mr. Spilka was born in New York City, and he studied at the Art Students League. He has also studied drawing with Rico Lebrun and sculpture with John Hovannes. Mr. Spilka enjoys traveling and has visited Belgium, England, France, and Luxembourg. He lives and works in New York City.